SEBASTIAN ROOK

VAMPIRE

Plagues

Jack blinked and stared at the inscription. Yes, something *was* happening! Cracks had begun to appear in the red plaster. Fine lines chased each other quickly across the surface.

And then Jack noticed something else: a faint plume of charcoal-grey was seeping through the cracks in the wall. Black shadows, like wisps of smoke, were trickling from behind the inscription!

Jack glanced at the next wall and then the next, his gaze darting around the octagonal chamber.

Slowly but surely, each wall was being obscured by dense, velvety-black shadow. Count Casimir Lampirska and his barons were coming. . .

Look out for...

Vampire Plagues 1: London
Vampire Plagues 2: Paris
Vampire Plagues 3: Mexico
Vampire Plagues 4: Outbreak
Vampire Plagues 5: Epidemic

SEBASTIAN ROOK

VAMPIRE Plagues

---◆---

EXTERMINATION

---◆---

■ SCHOLASTIC

With special thanks to Helen Hart

*For Tom Dyakowski and Milka Cichocka who kindly
helped with the Polish translations*

Scholastic Children's Books,
Euston House, 24 Eversholt Street,
London, NW1 1DB, UK
a division of Scholastic Ltd
London ~ New York ~ Toronto ~ Sydney ~ Auckland
Mexico City ~ New Delhi ~ Hong Kong

First published in the UK by Scholastic Ltd, 2006
Series created by Working Partners Ltd

Typeset by Falcon Oast Graphic Art Ltd
Printed and bound by Nørhaven Paperback A/S, Denmark

10 9 8 7 6 5 4 3 2 1

CHAPTER ONE

WARSAW, JANUARY 1851

The late afternoon sun hung low in the sky by the time the horse-drawn carriage finally rattled to a halt just inside the old city walls. Imposing watchtowers and tall turrets cast long shadows across the snowy street. Tallest of all the buildings set into the walls was the Monastery of St Wenceslaus. Its red stone walls and green onion-domed rooftops were strung with icicles which glittered in the fading daylight.

First out of the carriage door was Benedict Cole. He leaped down the steps, his leather boots striking the icy cobbles sharply. A tall, serious-looking boy who appeared older than his twelve years, Ben was wearing a grey coat with a black velvet collar, grey trousers, and thick black gloves. A freezing wind whipped along the street and tugged at his fair hair, making him shiver as he turned to help his sister Emily out of the carriage.

1

"Watch how you go, Em," he told her. "It's a bit slippery just here."

"Thank you," Emily said, placing her gloved hand in his as she carefully stepped down beside him.

At thirteen, Emily Cole was just ten months older than her brother, but quite a bit shorter. Because of the icy Warsaw winter, she was swathed from the tip of her nose to the tops of her boots in a warm, black coat. Her long auburn hair tumbled over her shoulders, framing her oval face as she smiled up at Ben.

Behind them, Jack Harkett sprang nimbly down from the carriage, his heavy wool jacket hanging loosely on his wiry frame. Not long ago, Jack had been a penniless orphan living on his wits on London's docks. But he had joined forces with Ben and Emily to fight a vampire plague.

That adventure had taken the three friends to Paris and Mexico, where they had battled against and finally defeated an ancient demon-god and his vampire servants. Recently, however, a new evil had arisen, and a different kind of vampire called a "lampir" had brought the friends to Poland.

Now, they all waited as the Coles' godfather, the eminent archaeologist and explorer Edwin Sherwood, went round to the front of the carriage to pay the driver. "Uncle" Edwin, as Ben and Emily called him, tucked his black stovepipe hat under one arm as he counted out the unfamiliar Polish coins.

He was a tall, lean man with greying hair. Since the death of their father, his best friend, Edwin had looked after Ben and Emily, and now Jack, too.

Eventually the carriage clattered away down the street, lurching as it rounded the corner at a trot. Edwin came across the street to join the three friends in front of the monastery.

"I ain't looking forward to this," Jack muttered, jamming his hands deep into his coat pockets. "Any funeral would be bad enough. But to be going to Filip's. . ." He broke off, shaking his head, and Ben patted his shoulder sympathetically.

The funeral was for their great friend and companion, Filip Cinska, who had helped the friends defeat a vicious army of blood-sucking lampirs. Just as victory had been within their grasp, Filip had been killed. His own brother, Doctor Roman Cinska, had fallen prey to evil forces. As a result he had become a half-lampir, half-human hybrid who would stop at nothing to prevent his brother and three friends from defeating the lampirs! Three days ago, Roman had thrown a knife intended for Emily's heart. But Filip had leaped in front of her and taken the blade in his own chest.

Now Ben, Jack and Emily had come to say goodbye to their friend for the last time. Filip was to be buried with honour in the grounds of the Monastery of St Wenceslaus, and the funeral would take place at sunset, the hour of his death.

"I'm not looking forward to it, either," Ben sighed, glancing at the pair of heavy oak doors which guarded the entrance to the monastery. "But at least we know that Filip didn't die in vain. If he hadn't saved Emily, then she would never have been able to finish the ritual – and we'd still have lampirs in the city!"

All four looked at each other soberly.

"We couldn't have done it without Filip," Emily agreed.

Ahead of them, one of the heavy oak doors suddenly swung open as if someone had been watching for the friends' arrival. A young monk wearing a thick brown cloak appeared in the doorway, his rosy cheeks glowing in the cold. His thatch of gingery hair had been shaved into a traditional monk's tonsure around a crown of pale pink scalp.

"Brother Lubek!" Ben cried, feeling his spirits lift slightly as he hurried forward to greet the monk, who had fought alongside him during their recent battles against the Warsaw lampirs. Young Brother Lubek had learned several languages during his time at the monastery, including English, and he had quickly become good friends with Ben, Jack and Emily.

Behind Brother Lubek stood the bright-eyed, portly abbot. A small wooden cross hung from his belt on a length of knotted cord and he had a leather-bound prayer book tucked under one arm.

"Good afternoon, Father Zachariasz," Edwin

Sherwood said, stepping forward to shake the abbot's hand. "How are you?"

"Good afternoon to you, Mister Sherwood," Father Zachariasz said in strongly-accented English. He beamed at Ben, Jack and Emily, then briskly ushered them all inside the monastery before closing the heavy oak doors tightly behind them. He spent a moment checking the locks and making sure that the doors were secure.

"Surely there ain't no need for that now, Father?" Jack said.

"Why would you say such a thing, Master Jack?" Father Zachariasz asked, looking puzzled.

"Because all the lampirs in the city have been destroyed," Jack replied with a shrug.

The abbot's smile faded. "Then you have not heard the news. . . ?" he said sadly.

"What news?" Ben asked quickly.

"The House of Wenceslaus was attacked last night," Father Zachariasz replied. "By lampirs!"

"*Lampirs?*" the three friends chorused in amazement. Ben saw that Emily had turned pale.

"But all the lampirs have been defeated," Ben said. The friends had walked in a circle around the city, ringing the Dhampir Bell and chanting the incantation which would seal the Warsaw lampirs in their graves. Ben's feet still ached from that day's work.

"The lampirs *inside* the city have been defeated,"

Father Zachariasz acknowledged with a nod. "But these came from outside Warsaw, my son. From outside the circle created by the ritual with the bell."

"They threw ropes and ladders fashioned from forest wood up against the wall," Brother Lubek put in. "We pushed the tops of the ladders backwards and made them fall. But we weren't fast enough to stop all the lampirs. About a dozen managed to climb over and drop down into the cloister garden. They were armed with knives and hammers."

"But *we* had fire," Father Zachariasz said, turning to Edwin Sherwood. "And I don't need to tell you, Mister Sherwood, what a deadly weapon that is in the fight against lampirs!"

"You most certainly don't," Edwin agreed. "Those creatures burn like dry tinder."

Edwin fell into step with Father Zachariasz and the two men began to make their way across the open courtyard towards a crumbling stone arch which led through to the cloister garden. Ben, Jack, Emily and Brother Lubek followed more slowly. The monastery buildings towered around them, the domed rooftops striped with fire by the late afternoon sun.

"I wonder what those lampirs wanted?" Emily said thoughtfully.

"More victims, of course," Brother Lubek replied.

But Emily shook her head. "If blood was all they wanted, they could have just walked straight into the city and attacked the first passer-by they came across. And we know that they didn't do that, because a fresh lampir attack would have been front page news." She frowned. "Why would those creatures go to the bother of making ladders and climbing such high walls?"

"Revenge?" suggested Jack.

"I've got a feeling it has something to do with Doctor Roman Cinska," Ben murmured.

Emily and Jack exchanged an exasperated glance, and Ben knew they were thinking about the argument which had raged between the three of them over the last few days. Emily and Jack were both convinced that the evil Doctor Roman had been defeated along with all the other lampirs in Warsaw. But a few nights ago, Ben was sure he had seen Roman standing on the other side of the street, watching them all.

"Ben, we've been over this," Emily sighed. "Roman Cinska is dead!"

"No. He's alive," Ben insisted, shaking his head. "I saw him!"

"You just *thought* you saw him, mate," Jack said in a soothing voice. "But you can't have done. He was defeated along with all the other lampirs in Warsaw. The Dhampir Bell saw to that!"

"But what if the bell didn't work on Roman?" Ben demanded. "The explosion in his laboratory meant he got an accidental dose of his lampir-antidote, and that made him half-lampir – but *only half*-lampir! It's

7

possible that the ritual wasn't as effective on him as it was on the ordinary lampirs."

There was a silence as they all considered this. Eventually Jack said, "You've got a point there, mate."

Emily nodded. "We don't know whether that is the case," she pointed out sensibly. "But *if* it is, and *if* Roman is still alive, then we'll have to find another way to defeat him."

"I just hope it's as simple as that," Ben muttered as they all followed Edwin and Father Zachariasz through the crumbling stone archway. "But I have a nasty feeling that destroying Doctor Roman Cinska is not going to be easy!"

As Emily stepped into the cloister garden, she was struck by the change in the place since she'd first visited the monastery a little over a week ago. Then the gardens had been green and full of herbs. Now, almost everywhere she looked, Emily saw burnt stubble and fire-blackened stone. She could still smell the smoke, and knew that if she closed her eyes she would see flames in her mind's eye.

Three nights ago, she had watched from the doorway of the little chapel in the middle of the cloisters as Ben and Jack had each seized an oil lamp and set fire to the gardens. Dozens of lampirs had been sent to their doom, and dozens more had been destroyed during a great battle which had raged until dawn.

So much had happened since then, culminating in Filip's heroic sacrifice. . .

And now here was Filip's coffin, being carried out of the chapel on the shoulders of six monks in hooded robes. The little procession came to a halt in front of Father Zachariasz, who glanced up at the sky. The sun was dark red, so low now that it seemed to rest on the rooftops.

The abbot nodded. "It is almost sunset," he said gently. "I believe it is time to begin." Turning to Brother Lubek, he added, "Would you be so kind as to fetch the bell?"

Brother Lubek nodded and disappeared inside the chapel, his robes swirling around his sandalled feet.

"Do you mean the Dhampir Bell?" Emily asked curiously.

"I do indeed, Miss Emily," Father Zachariasz confirmed. "The bell is still here safe and sound, its clapper carefully wrapped in fabric, so that the bell cannot be rung accidentally." He nodded and clasped his hands across his round stomach. "And now I have arranged for the Dhampir Bell to be buried with Filip. He was its guardian for the last few weeks of his life – he even followed it to England and brought it back home – so it is only fitting that he should guard it in death, now that the bell's work is done."

The sun slipped lower in the west, turning the rooftops to a blaze of red and orange. Shadows gathered and a chill breeze whispered through the cloister garden.

Brother Lubek emerged from the doorway of the little chapel. Clasped in his arms was a large bronze dome, its curved rim intricately carved with symbols.

As the young monk made his way towards them, Emily, remembering Ben's doubts, felt a tremor of misgiving. *Is the Dhampir Bell's work really done?* she wondered. And if it was, then surely it would be better to destroy the bell entirely, so that there was no risk of lampirs ever taking control of its power as they had tried to do in London.

"Father Zachariasz, are you sure that burying the Dhampir Bell is the best thing?" she asked hesitantly.

"I am absolutely sure," the abbot replied firmly. "And this afternoon, only one question remains – who should be the one to position the bell upon Filip's casket during the funeral ceremony?"

Emily saw Ben and Jack glance at her.

"Emily?" Ben asked gently.

She shook her head. "I think it should be Jack," she murmured.

"That's a fine idea," Edwin Sherwood said. "Filip would have wanted you to do it, Jack."

Jack blushed. "All right then," he said quietly.

The sun set just as Jack stepped forwards to take his position beside Filip Cinska's burial casket. Beyond it yawned the open grave, and Jack could see Ben and

Emily on the far side, standing with their heads bowed. Behind them was a sombre Edwin Sherwood, tall and lean in his long black coat, his stovepipe hat clasped in front of him.

Feeling slightly nervous, Jack tightened his grip on the Dhampir Bell. The large bronze dome gleamed as he looked at it, reflecting the flickering, golden light of the four flaming torches that stood around the grave.

Father Zachariasz was reading the words of the burial service. "You were created from ashes, and you will return to ash. . ."

The sky was deepening to a dusky blue and Brother Lubek stood at the abbot's side, holding aloft a flaming torch so that Father Zachariasz could read from his prayer book.

Standing in a big circle all around the funeral group were a dozen or so monks, in the rust-coloured robes of the Monastery of St Wenceslaus. Their thick hoods were pulled forwards against the cold, so that the men's faces were in deep shadow. Jack could just make out several more monks coming slowly across the cloister garden. They had their hands tucked inside their sleeves, and their hooded heads were bowed in prayer.

"Rest in peace. . ." Father Zachariasz intoned. He made the sign of the cross over Filip's casket with his right hand, and then nodded at Jack.

It was time to position the Dhampir Bell.

A square of purple velvet had been draped across the

centre of the casket, and Jack knew that he was to place the Dhampir Bell carefully on top of it. Six monks would then slowly lower Filip's coffin into the grave on silken cords.

Twilight deepened. An icy gust of wind seemed to come from nowhere, making the monks' robes billow. It stirred the thatch on the rooftops of the outbuildings at the far end of the cloister garden. The flaming torches guttered briefly and then flared again, throwing dancing shadows against the walls of the nearby chapel.

Jack reached forwards, the bell clasped so tightly in his extended hands that he could see its patterned rim shaking slightly. He was aware of movement on his left as several monks stepped closer to the grave. Jack knew that as soon as he had positioned the bell, these monks would lift the silken cords and begin to lower the casket, hand over hand. He and his friends would say goodbye to Filip for ever. . .

But just then, the nearest monk threw back his thick hood with one hand. Jack caught a glimpse of strange, milky-white eyes, and his heart began to race. He saw the next monk tear back his hood . . . and then the next . . . and the next.

Beneath their hoods, the monks' faces were blotchy and purplish, their skin starting to peel in places. Razor-sharp fangs glittered in the torchlight – and Jack knew with a sickening certainty that these were not monks at all, but the undead: lampirs!

And they had come for the bell.

CHAPTER TWO

"Lampirs!" Ben shouted.

His heart pounding, he made a frantic grab for one of the torches. He could feel the scorching heat from the flames as he jerked it out of the ground.

Desperately Ben jabbed the torch at the nearest lampir. The creature had once been a man, tall and strong with powerful shoulders beneath his monk's-robe disguise. But now he was undead, and his dry flesh ignited easily. Bright fire engulfed him as he staggered backwards away from Ben, and his hideous, half-rotten face twisted in agony. Soon all that was left was a column of silvery-black ash which abruptly collapsed in on itself. The lampir was dead.

"Nice work, Ben!" shouted Edwin as he hurled his hat to the ground and made a grab for another of the flaming torches. A lampir lunged at him, but Edwin swung the torch in front of him like a sword and the creature howled in fury. It was a woman, Ben saw, her honey-brown hair piled high and pinned with silver clips. She was armed with a knife that she'd been hiding in the folds of her robe, and the blade glittered as she slashed at Edwin.

But Edwin moved fast. He ducked down, swinging his torch low to the ground so that the flames licked the hem of her robe. The flames quickly took hold, and the woman screeched as the blaze engulfed her.

Looking stunned at the turn of events, Father Zachariasz reached for the nearest torch, while several of the real monks fled across the cloister garden, screaming in terror.

"The lampirs are after the Dhampir Bell!" yelled Emily.

Ben followed his sister's gaze and saw that one of the creatures, a man, was heading straight for Jack. The lampir had torn off his monk's robes to reveal a skeletal body hung with remnants of ragged clothing. Rotted leaves and moss clung to his thin black hair.

Appalled, Ben darted forwards. But he was forced to stop abruptly because the open grave yawned at his feet. He looked up across the chasm in horror as the lampir got to Jack first.

The lampir hissed and tried to knock the Dhampir Bell out of Jack's hands. Ben saw his friend clasp the bell tightly to his chest and ward the creature off with one outstretched hand. . .

And the lampir backed away!

Ben saw a flash of gold on Jack's middle finger and guessed immediately what had happened. Not long ago, the friends had found a legend in the Dhampir Tome, an old book hidden for centuries in the scriptorium of the monastery. The legend had said that if someone wore a piece of jewellery which had belonged to a victim of lampir plague, then the wearer would be protected from lampir attack. And Jack had just such a piece of jewellery – a wedding ring left to him by an old friend called Molly, whose grandmother had died of lampir plague in London.

The ring had proved invaluable in their fight against lampirs, protecting Jack at every turn. And now, Ben was relieved to see, it was working its magic again.

But, unfortunately, Jack was the only person with such a ring. And right now, Ben could see that it was Emily who was in danger! She had rushed to the foot of the grave and was desperately tugging the last of the flaming torches out of the ground. But behind her was a lampir – a young man, not long dead, with a fresh bloom to his waxy cheeks as if the undertaker had used rouge to give the lifeless face colour.

The lampir was still wearing his monk's robes, and the brown fabric rippled as he raised a wooden club and prepared to strike Emily a crushing blow on the back of her head.

"Em, behind you!" Ben yelled as he launched himself towards his sister's attacker.

Emily twisted round, wrenching the torch from the ground, just in time to swing it upwards with enough force to bury the burning tip in the lampir's stomach. The creature howled and dropped the club. The thick brown fabric of the monk's robes quickly caught alight and soon the lampir was a mass of crackling flames.

"Well done, Em!" Ben cried, and turned to see where the next threat was coming from.

It was a terrifying sight. Lampirs were everywhere, snarling and gnashing their fangs. And then Ben caught a glimpse of a colossal figure, rearing up out of the gathering shadows. Impossibly tall – easily over two metres – and clad from head to foot in a cowled robe, the creature had a cadaverous white face and steely blue eyes which seemed to burn Ben as he was briefly caught in their gaze.

Ben blinked as the figure pushed back its hood. Orange torchlight played across the face of Doctor Roman Cinska: half-human, half-lampir, wholly evil.

"Give up the Dhampir Bell, Jack Harkett – you cannot fight me now!" Roman snarled.

"You reckon?" Jack yelled, and across the grave Ben saw his friend square his shoulders bravely. "I've fought bigger demons than you, Doctor!"

Roman Cinska growled deep in his throat. His eyes blazed. "Give up the bell, you miserable little worm," he snarled.

"Worm, am I? Bet you ain't never seen a worm

wearing one o' these!" Jack shouted, holding up his hand so that Roman Cinska could clearly see the gold ring on his middle finger.

Then, with a yell, Jack leaped forwards as if he was going to punch Doctor Cinska on the jaw. But just before his fist connected, Roman hissed and jerked away, his robes rippling as he flung up an arm to protect himself.

Ben gripped his flaming torch firmly and exchanged a glance with Edwin, who nodded grimly.

"Ready when you are, Ben," said the archaeologist.

"Now!" Ben cried, and simultaneously, Ben and Edwin rushed around the grave and stabbed their torches at Roman.

With a howl, the evil doctor staggered backwards. His black form seemed to shimmer and fade, and abruptly he vanished. The two flaming torches clashed together in mid-air, sending out a shower of sparks which landed on the thatched roof of a nearby outbuilding. The thatch began to smoulder.

"The doctor has resorted to shadow-form!" Brother Lubek shouted, as an inky black shape rippled away across the earth. "He knows he's safe like that. We can't set fire to mere shadow!"

Ben cried out in frustration, but there were lampirs in human-form all around him and he was forced to fight. He jabbed his torch at a skeletal man who approached from his right. The lampir caught fire immediately and burned fast, a twisting pillar of fire. The night air was filled with the smell of smoke and charred flesh. One of the outbuildings was ablaze now, flames licking fiercely across its thatched roof.

More lampirs came lurching out of the shadows, fighting to reach the Dhampir Bell.

"We're outnumbered," Edwin yelled.

"And Roman Cinska is still here somewhere," Jack pointed out grimly. "Though the fire may drive 'im off!" he added.

Ben looked around at the inferno that was growing at an alarming rate and now threatened to consume the entire monastery.

"We must flee the monastery!" Father Zachariasz cried, his quick gaze darting from one lampir to the next, and then to the encroaching flames. "We cannot hope to fight so many and win, and if the lampirs do not kill us, the fire will!"

"This way!" Brother Lubek shouted urgently. He held his torch high over his head, giving them all a beacon to follow as he darted across the cloister garden, weaving a path which led away from the lampirs.

Jack, Emily and Father Zachariasz quickly followed, while Ben stood shoulder-to-shoulder with Edwin. Together they swiped the air with their flaming torches, keeping the lampirs at bay so that everyone could escape. A chill breeze made the torches flare wildly. Nearby, there was a cracking sound as the burning roof of the thatched outbuilding suddenly collapsed. Bright flames and a plume of orange sparks hurtled up into the darkness and the lampirs cowered, hissing with fear.

One of them, however, was more reckless than his comrades. He was a thick-set man with a long, black beard which curled to his waist. Fresh from the grave, his flesh had begun to rot and part of his cheek was missing, revealing white bone and razor-sharp fangs beneath. He loped towards Ben and Edwin, and the stench of rotting flesh came off him in waves.

"Get back!" Ben yelled, and swung his torch in a flaring arc which caught the lampir-man beneath his beard. The black hair crackled as the flames took hold, and the bitter stench of burning hair and flesh caught at Ben's nostrils as the creature burned.

"Come on, Ben. The others are safe now. Let's get out of here!" urged Edwin.

"We'd better make sure the lampirs can't follow," Ben said grimly.

Together they threw their torches at the crowd of lampirs that surged towards them. The ones in front immediately went up in flames, forming an effective, fiery barrier between the friends and the remaining lampirs.

"This way!" came Emily's voice.

Ben glanced over his shoulder and saw that she was standing in front of a stone archway. Jack was beside her, the Dhampir Bell cradled in his arms.

Ben ran towards them. Edwin was right behind him.

Howls of rage ripped the air as the lampirs found themselves unable to follow.

The blaze was spreading quickly now, fanned by the breeze. Bright fire-balls leaped from one outbuilding to the next. In one of the tall, domed towers, a bell began to ring frantically, signalling the monastery's distress across the city.

Out in the courtyard, Ben saw immediately that other monks had gathered, some clutching baskets and bundles of items they had saved from the fire. Some were talking in rapid Polish to Father Zachariasz.

"What is it?" asked Ben, turning to Brother Lubek. "What are they saying?"

"They have just come from the hospital wing where the dead bodies of several of our brethren have just been discovered," the young monk replied. "They seem to have been slaughtered earlier this evening, their throats slashed and the flesh torn from their bones." He shook his head in disbelief. "Brother Tomasz is saying that for some reason the bodies were stripped of their clothes."

"I reckon they were killed for their robes," Jack muttered. "That's where the lampirs got all those hooded cloaks from!"

"We have to get out of here," Emily said, glancing back over her shoulder. "The fire's spreading!" Flames were licking across the courtyard towards them. High above, a flickering red glow lit up the sky.

Brother Lubek crossed the courtyard and dragged

open the heavy oak doors. Ben caught a glimpse of the street beyond, where people had gathered to gape at the burning monastery in disbelief.

"Come on!" Ben grabbed Emily's hand and together they raced through the doorway with Jack, Edwin and Father Zachariasz at their heels.

"*Pozar!*" Emily could hear the word shouted over and over again. *Fire!*

The Monastery of St Wenceslaus was now a blazing inferno. Huge red sparks spiralled up into the night sky, flames licked at the rooftops, and there was a thunderous crash as something collapsed. Somewhere another bell was clanging. More onlookers were rushing to the scene, bellowing, "*Pozar! Pozar!*" Men and women from nearby houses carried buckets of water, passing them hand-to-hand.

"The scriptorium!" Father Zachariasz suddenly cried. "I must go back in and save the books ... the manuscripts!" He wheeled round and made as if to rush back into the monastery, but Ben and Brother Lubek quickly held him back.

"But I must save the books ... and the Dhampir Tome!" Father Zachariasz wailed in despair.

Anxiously, Emily turned to look back at the monastery. If the Dhampir Tome burned, then centuries of knowledge about fighting lampirs would be lost for ever.

"The scriptorium is in a stone building," Brother Lubek said reassuringly. "Fire may blacken the outside walls, but it will never touch the inside."

Emily heard the sound of glass exploding in the heat, and felt a sudden scorching blast of hot air on her cheeks. "We should move further away," she said.

Guided by Edwin and Brother Lubek, the group began to make their way along the cobbled street.

"This is a catastrophe," muttered Father Zachariasz, glancing back at the monastery. The abbot's face was haggard with despair, his robes stained with soot. "So many precious things lost. So many of the brethren made homeless. I am not sure what to do now. . ."

"You'll come back to the hotel with us, of course," Edwin said firmly.

Emily joined Ben and Jack. "It seems you were right, Ben," she said quietly, linking arms with her brother. "The ritual didn't work on Doctor Roman Cinska. He is still alive and well – and extremely dangerous!"

CHAPTER THREE

It was late by the time they all got to the hotel, and news of the fire had already reached the staff. Wide-eyed bell-boys waited to escort refugees to spare bedrooms, and hot Polish tea was pressed on everyone who came through the doors.

Until recently, the friends had all been sharing Edwin Sherwood's room, since the hotel was full of people attending the Royal Symposium of Archaeology and Anthropology – a conference at which Edwin himself had been a key speaker. Now that the symposium was over, however, the friends had rooms of their own at last. But, even so, they all slept fitfully that night, unsettled by the evening's events.

Early the next morning the friends gathered in Edwin Sherwood's hotel room before breakfast to discuss what should be done about the Dhampir Bell. Emily was perched on a chair by the writing table, her hands folded in her lap as she watched Jack and Ben pace up and down the room. Both boys were deep in thought.

"We can't risk having Roman Cinska get his hands on the Dhampir Bell," Jack said at last. "He'll use it to reawaken the lampirs we defeated!"

"I still think we should bury it," Father Zachariasz said firmly. He was sitting on a leather couch on the other side of the room, his face drawn and tired. Emily guessed that he probably hadn't slept much. "If the bell is far underground," he went on, "then no lampir can lay a finger on it. But we will all know where it is, if we ever need to use it again."

"What's to stop the lampirs digging it up?" Ben asked. "We know how organized they are, now that Roman's in charge."

Edwin was standing by the window, holding the white lace curtain back with one hand as he gazed down into Warsaw's elegant Castle Square. "I'm afraid Ben's right," he said, turning round to look at them all. "The bell wouldn't last two minutes if we buried it."

"Then what about the scriptorium?" Brother Lubek asked. "The Dhampir Tome was hidden there for centuries. Even we monks didn't know it was there! Perhaps we could hide the bell there for centuries to come?"

"But you'd have to guard it day and night," Jack pointed out.

"I've got an idea," Emily said. She glanced at the others and added, "I don't know if you'll like it, though."

"Go on, Em," Ben urged.

"We take the Dhampir Bell back to the foundry where the new clapper was made last week," she said. "And we ask our friend Ivo to melt it down."

There was a moment of silence. Nobody moved.

"*Melt it down. . . ?*" Father Zachariasz repeated in a shocked voice. "You are not serious, Emily, my dear?"

"I most certainly am!" Emily said firmly. "Melting the bell is the only way to be sure that Roman and his lampirs can never get their claws on it."

"But to destroy a thing of such ancient power and beauty," Father Zachariasz gasped. "That would be sacrilege!"

"Sacrilege or not, I think Em's right," Jack said. He had stopped pacing and was now standing by the door with his hands in his pockets, nodding vigorously. "The Dhampir Bell has to be destroyed. Last night's fight was a close thing. If I hadn't been wearing Molly's ring, who knows what would have happened?"

"Roman Cinska would be out there using the Dhampir Bell to build himself another army," Ben said grimly.

Father Zachariasz sighed. "Maybe you're right. . ." he said, his shoulders drooping.

Just then, there was a knock at the door and Jack opened it cautiously. A cheerful bell-boy in a blue jacket grinned and held out a large silver tray piled high with Polish sweet pastries and tall tea-glasses.

"Breakfast," Edwin said. "And today's newspapers, I see." He cleared a space on a small table by the window so that the bell-boy could put the tray down. "I wonder whether there are any reports of last night's fire?"

"The early morning edition of the Warsaw *Record*," Brother Lubek said, taking one of the newspapers.

The young monk scanned the front page, nodding to himself. "Here we are. . ." he said eventually, frowning slightly as he translated from Polish for them. " 'Inferno at Monastery. Ten believed dead.' "

"Ten?" Jack said, checking that the door was closed behind the bell-boy. "I suppose that'll be those poor monks we found in the courtyard."

"We were lucky that the death toll was not higher," Father Zachariasz said soberly. "Many of the brethren were out in the city yesterday, ministering to the poor. Their absence will have saved their lives."

Ben helped Edwin to pass round plates and tea-glasses. "What else does the report say?" he asked Brother Lubek.

" 'The blaze was attended by fifty men from Warsaw's new voluntary fire-service'. . ." the young monk said, frowning a little as he translated. "'The fire was well-established by they time they arrived and all the wooden sections of the monastery were destroyed, but they used water-pumps to fight and finally extinguish the blaze. . . The cause of the fire remains a mystery'. . ."

Father Zachariasz briskly drained his tea-glass.

"I shall return to the monastery with all haste," he said decisively. "There are decisions to be made, and plans to put into action. We must rebuild the house of St Wenceslaus and continue our charitable works. We shall need builders and tilers and thatchers."

"What about the Dhampir Bell. . . ?" Emily prompted.

"Of course you must melt it," Father Zachariasz said sadly. "After the events of last night, I have given this matter a lot of thought. Unfortunately, I think you are right, Emily. The bell must be put beyond Roman Cinska's reach. For ever."

Once they had said goodbye to Father Zachariasz and Brother Lubek, the friends put on their coats and prepared to go to Ivo's foundry. Ben carefully wrapped the Dhampir Bell in a pillowcase and solemnly handed it to Jack.

They left Edwin Sherwood sitting at his desk.

"The daylight means you'll be safe from lampirs," the archaeologist said. "If you don't mind, I shall stay here and begin making the arrangements for our journey home to England."

Outside the hotel, the three friends flagged down a four-seater "Berlin" carriage, which rattled them eastwards along wide boulevards lined with colourful terraced houses painted custard-yellow and duck-egg blue.

The foundry was in a small brick warehouse beside

the Wisla, a wide river which cut the city of Warsaw neatly in half. Ben hammered on the door with his fist.

A few moments later, the door creaked open and Ben smiled when he saw Ivo's familiar face peering out. He was only a year or two older than the friends, with dirty-yellow hair and a turned-up nose. His small, skinny frame was swamped by a big brown leather apron and his hands were black with soot.

"Hello, Ivo!" Ben said. "Remember us?"

"*Tak, tak!*" Ivo said, grinning cheerfully. "*Yes, yes!* I remember – you bring bell before."

The young apprentice threw the door wide open and beckoned them in. "You will please come in," he said in heavily-accented English. "My master, he gone. . ." and Ivo flapped a hand in the direction of a nearby tavern. The windows were open, and drunken laughter echoed from within. "He not back until later."

The three friends followed Ivo through a stout oak door. Beyond was the foundry – a huge barn-like room with a fiery forge in the middle. An enormous blackened funnel acted as a chimney above it, and a variety of small cranks, cranes and pulleys were assembled on either side.

Ivo turned to the friends. "How am I helping you?" he asked. His gaze fell on Jack's pillowcase-wrapped bundle. "You are bringing bell again!"

"That's right," said Ben with a quick nod. "But this time we want you to melt it down."

Ben gestured to Jack, who quickly unwrapped the Dhampir Bell and placed it on a nearby workbench. They all stared at its gleaming bronze curves for a moment.

"You are wanting to *melt* the bell. . ." Ivo said hesitantly. "You would destroy such a beautiful thing?" He looked as though he couldn't quite believe what he was hearing.

"That's right," Emily put in with a firm nod. "We *have* to destroy it. It's too dangerous." She moved towards the apprentice and gently touched his sleeve. "You've seen the power of the Dhampir Bell, Ivo, and so you know what it can do. We can't risk having it stolen by the enemy and used for evil."

A few days ago, Ivo had walked around Warsaw with the friends and witnessed the ritual. Now he nodded sombrely. "I will melt it," he said flatly.

Without further ado, the apprentice adjusted his leather apron and made his way over to the forge. He applied a pair of bellows to the fire until it glowed white-hot. The air in the room felt scorching. Ben could barely breathe. He shrugged off his coat, and Jack did the same, while Emily grinned and fanned herself with her gloves.

Ivo crossed the room to where a row of blackened instruments hung from a rack on the wall. He selected what looked to Ben like an enormous ceramic cauldron, and attached it to a length of chain hanging down over the fire.

Then Ben cautiously removed the fabric from around the clapper of the Dhampir Bell, and together, he and Ivo placed the bell in the ceramic cauldron, taking care that the clapper never touched the sides of the bell. Finally, with a slow and careful twist of a lever, the cauldron was lowered into the glowing forge.

For a long time, nothing happened. Ben began to worry that the Dhampir Bell was protected in some way, perhaps by the same kind of enchantment that made the bell so powerful in the fight against lampirs. He exchanged a couple of anxious glances with Jack and Emily.

But eventually the bronze surface of the bell began to darken and shimmer. The inscriptions around the rim grew indistinct.

"It's melting," Emily murmured, her voice full of awe and a little relief.

Slowly, the Dhampir Bell liquefied into hot, fluid bronze.

At last Ivo swiped the back of his wrist across his sweating face and turned to the three friends with a wide grin. "Is done," he said simply.

The friends moved forwards and peered into the crucible to see the deep pool of shimmering liquid bronze. The Dhampir Bell was gone.

The three friends looked at each other. No one knew quite what to say.

Behind them, the stout oak door suddenly flew open

and a young lad came hurtling into the room, gabbling excitedly in Polish. He pulled himself up when he saw Ben, Jack and Emily, and gazed uncertainly at them.

The newcomer was about the same age as Ivo, with brown hair that stuck up in spikes.

"Kaspar!" cried Ivo with a grin.

"Ivo!" Kaspar exclaimed, and immediately launched into rapid Polish again, his eyes wide and his hands gesticulating wildly. He waved his arms, widened his eyes, and then clasped his hands together as if he was holding a pistol or a musket. He spoke so fast that he tripped over some of his words, finally coming to a breathless finish.

Ben couldn't begin to imagine what he'd said, but it had obviously impressed Ivo, whose eyes were now like saucers.

"What's happening, mate?" Jack asked Ivo. "What's going on?"

Ivo seemed to struggle to find the words in English. "My friend Kaspar, he works as groom at inn," he said at last. "Kaspar say stagecoach full of important men leave Warsaw at night. Out on lonely road, bad man come. . ." he hesitated, frowning as he tried to translate. "Bad man . . . with pistol. He shoot passengers."

"He means a bandit," Emily said, understanding. "A highwayman!"

Kaspar nodded excitedly. "High. Way. Man," he said eagerly, and clasped his hands together, pointing his fingers to make the shape of a pistol. Then he stood on tiptoes to make himself as tall as possible, talking in rapid-fire Polish all the while.

"He is big, bad man," Ivo translated hesitantly. "Very, *very* big! And he has white face. And eyes that burn like . . . like forge!"

Ben felt his heart begin to pound. He glanced at Emily and Jack, and knew by the stunned looks on their faces that they were thinking exactly what he was.

An impossibly tall highwayman, with a white face and eyes that burned? There was one person they all knew who fitted that description: Doctor Roman Cinska!

CHAPTER FOUR

"The highwayman has to be Roman," Ben said flatly. "What's he up to?"

The three friends looked at each other soberly for a moment, then Jack turned to Ivo. "Can you ask Kaspar where this happened?" he asked.

"It would be useful to know if there were any survivors," Emily put in quickly.

Ivo and Kaspar talked quickly in Polish for a few moments. Then Ivo translated for the friends. "He say this happen a short way outside city walls. One man – he still alive. He injured, but he come back to Warsaw – to inn where Kaspar is feeding horses. The innkeeper send Kaspar for doctor. Kaspar call at house of doctor, then come here to tell his friend." He patted his own chest proudly to show that he was Kaspar's friend.

Jack glanced at Ben and Emily. "We should go and see this fellow," he said urgently.

"I agree," said Ben. "His story might give us some

clues about what Roman Cinska is up to." He turned to Ivo. "Would Kaspar take us to the inn?" he asked.

Kaspar shrugged and nodded.

"I come too!" Ivo put in eagerly.

"Good idea," Emily said. "If the man doesn't speak English, we'll need you to translate!"

The coaching inn was a few streets away, a long, low building with glossily-painted white shutters and a cobbled yard strewn with hay and straw. The innkeeper gave Kaspar an affectionate cuff round the ear for being so long on his errand, and then led the three friends and Ivo upstairs.

A portly man in a tweed waistcoat was just coming out of one of the rooms. He carried a large leather bag in one hand, and Jack guessed he must be the local doctor. The innkeeper exchanged a few quiet words with him, and then ushered the friends into a large, airy bedroom which overlooked the stables.

There was a four-poster bed in the middle of the room, its blue velvet drapes tied back neatly. A young girl was bending over the bed, bandaging the arm of a thin, white-faced man who winced and bit his lip. He had a graze across one cheek, and blood had begun to seep through the bandage already.

The friends hovered at the foot of the bed while Ivo spoke gently in Polish to the wounded man.

After a while the man replied, nodding and gritting his teeth.

"This is Viktor Walenty," Ivo told the friends. "He is businessman travelling to Minsk. But he say stagecoach was held up by a highwayman with many pistols – one in each hand and three strapped to his chest. There was loud bang, and Viktor saw one of the passengers fall to the ground. He was frightened. . ." Ivo hesitated, searching for the right words as he translated what Viktor had told him. "He say there was much screaming and travellers tried to get out of carriage. Then, highwayman, he shoots while they are running away. Viktor sees others fall to the ground and knows they are dead! Then he feels pain in his shoulder and he falls. There is much blood on his shirt and he knows he is shot. So he pretend to be dead. He stay very still on the ground, and highwayman think everybody is killed."

"What happened next?" Emily asked anxiously.

Ivo spoke to Viktor again. "He say highwayman is wanting the stagecoach for himself," he said at last. "He ordered coachman to drive to village in south Poland."

"Any idea what the village is called?" queried Ben, and the friends waited once more while Ivo spoke quietly to Viktor.

"*Ornak!*" cried the wounded man, his face grey with pain. "*Ornak!*"

The girl had finished bandaging Viktor's arm. She stood up, and with a determined look on her face, firmly shooed the friends and Ivo towards the bedroom door.

"*Ornak. . . ?*" Ben repeated with a frown as they made

their way downstairs. "What does that mean, Ivo?"

"Ornak is name of small village," Ivo replied. "Very small place . . . far away in mountains."

The four emerged into the inn's bustling yard. A stagecoach had just arrived, and Kaspar was lugging a bucket of oats across to the horses.

"Now why would Roman Cinska want to go to a little village called Ornak?" Ben said thoughtfully.

They said goodbye to Ivo and Kaspar, and headed back to the hotel, rattling over the cobbles in a small carriage that Ben flagged down outside the coaching inn.

"I think I know why Roman's gone to Ornak," Emily said quietly, as the carriage set off.

Jack and Ben turned to her at once, their faces full of amazement.

"Why didn't you say so before?" Jack asked.

"I didn't want to talk about it in front of Ivo," she replied. "It's not good news."

"Go on, Em," Ben said encouragingly. "Tell us what you know."

"When Filip and I were translating the Dhampir Tome last week," she said, "we found a reference to Count Casimir Lampirska. He was the feudal lord of Ornak, and around four hundred years ago he and six evil barons began to dabble in the black arts. They held rituals in Count Casimir's castle, high in the mountains above Ornak."

"Rituals. . ." Jack muttered, staring out the window at the bustling streets of Warsaw. "Why don't I like the sound o' that?"

"They sacrificed children," Emily said flatly. "The Tome was full of stories about how the count and his barons stole young victims from the village of Ornak." She shuddered. "They drank the children's blood in a quest to give themselves eternal life."

"I remember Filip telling us about this," Ben said slowly. "By drinking human blood, the count and his barons became the first lampirs. Which means that Ornak is the birthplace of lampirism!"

"And Roman's going there," Jack muttered. "What's he up to?"

"There's only one way to find out," Emily said as the carriage clattered into Castle Square and drew up in front of the hotel.

Jack and Ben stared at her, and then glanced at each other.

"We have to go after him!" Jack exclaimed.

Ben nodded. "We need to find out what he's up to, and stop him," he agreed. Then he grinned. "I wonder whether Uncle Edwin has finished making our travel arrangements yet?" he said with a chuckle. "He'll be surprised to hear we're planning to go south instead of north."

The friends found Edwin Sherwood in his hotel room, pouring Polish tea into tall tea-glasses. Father Zachariasz and Brother Lubek had returned from the monastery and were telling him about the clear-up operation.

"Ah, you're back," Edwin said, greeting Emily, Jack and Ben with a smile.

"We're back," Emily confirmed with a nod. "The Dhampir Bell has been melted down, Uncle Edwin. And we've got some news about Roman Cinska. He attacked a stagecoach just before dawn. Most of the passengers were killed, but there was one man who escaped. We've been to see him. . ." Emily quickly told her godfather and the two monks everything that they had learned.

Father Zachariasz looked anxious. "What would Roman Cinska want in Ornak?" he muttered.

"That's exactly what we mean to find out," Emily said.

"And how do you intend to do that?" Edwin asked, but the expression on his face told Emily that her godfather had already guessed the answer.

"We're going to Ornak, of course!" Jack said with a grin.

Edwin sighed. "As if I needed to ask," he said.

"That is easier said than done, Jack," Father Zachariasz pointed out. "Ornak must be several days' journey, near the Tatra Mountains. And once you get there, how will you make yourselves understood? Ornak is not like Warsaw. I will be very surprised if you find a single person there who speaks English."

The three friends exchanged crestfallen glances.

"Father Zachariasz has a point," Jack muttered. "How will we ask for help if we need it?"

Emily bit her lip. "It was always Filip who translated for us," she said.

"Perhaps I could go with you," Brother Lubek suggested hesitantly. "After all, you will need a guide who knows the area. . ."

"Do *you* know the area?" Ben asked curiously.

Brother Lubek blushed. "I am from the city of Krakow," he said in a proud voice. "It is just north of the Tatra Mountains, and not far from Ornak."

"Well, ain't that a stroke of luck?" Jack murmured. "Now all we have to do is decide how we're going to travel."

"Could we go by stagecoach?" suggested Emily. "We'd pay our way, of course. We wouldn't steal one like Roman!"

But Brother Lubek shook his head. "Too slow. Horseback is faster," he said decisively. "And it will mean we can avoid the main highways. Believe me, everywhere south of Krakow is lampir territory. Even before Sir Peter Walker rang the Dhampir Bell and released those lampirs that had been trapped in their graves, there were sporadic outbreaks of lampir plague in the mountain villages. Since the ringing of the bell, there have been more lampir attacks than ever. The Warsaw lampirs may have been defeated, but there are thousands more away from the city, and I am certain they will have lookouts posted at every crossroads around Ornak."

"We definitely want to arrive without them knowing about us," Ben said.

"Just so," Brother Lubek agreed with a grin. "On horseback we can cut across country. We may even arrive before Roman Cinska does!"

"That would be marvellous," Emily said. "That way we can warn the people of Ornak."

Edwin pulled a fob-watch out of his waistcoat pocket and glanced at it. "It's almost noon," he said. "Let's get organized. We'll need to get on the road soon if we're to make the most of the daylight."

"But what about the practical considerations?" Father Zachariasz interrupted, looking worried. "For example, where will you find horses for hire at such short notice?"

"I saw plenty in the stables at the coaching inn," Jack said. "Perhaps if I go and talk to Kaspar, he could arrange something for us."

"I will come with you," Brother Lubek offered, and they headed for the door.

"And what about food. . . ?" Father Zachariasz said, wringing his hands.

"The hotel's head chef is a reasonable fellow," Edwin said, patting the abbot's shoulder in a reassuring way. "I'm sure he'll rustle up some supplies for us."

"And clothes for Brother Lubek. . . ?" Father Zachariasz added. "He cannot ride horseback in just his robes!"

"I can help out there," Ben said firmly. "I've got dozens of pairs of breeches."

Horses . . . food . . . clothes for the journey. . . Emily felt excitement ripple through her. They were going south to the mountains, hot on the trail of Doctor Roman Cinska. It seemed another adventure had begun!

CHAPTER FIVE

Just over an hour later, Ben made his way downstairs to the crowded hotel lobby, a canvas knapsack tucked under one arm. Edwin had said that they would need to travel light, so Ben had packed the bare essentials and left the rest in his room. Edwin had insisted that they keep their rooms at the hotel, ready for their return. It was more than a practical measure. It was a symbol of their determination to succeed and return to Warsaw.

Across the lobby he saw that a party of ladies had just arrived. The marble floor was awash with glossy hat-boxes and brightly-coloured leather valises. Bell-boys scampered this way and that, and Ben could just about make out Edwin's tall form over by the entrance to the dining room. His godfather was in deep conversation with one of the waiters, and Ben could see that parcels of food were being packed into a leather saddlebag.

Just then the hotel's double doors burst open and Jack rushed in with Brother Lubek.

42

"Five horses, all saddled and waitin' at the stables," Jack said with a grin. "Although my backside ain't looking forward to the ride, I can tell—" He broke off suddenly, eyes wide as he stared past Ben's shoulder.

Ben turned round, wondering what Jack was looking at. But all he could see was a young lad coming down the stairs, wearing a short jacket and breeches tucked into long leather boots. The lad was grinning, his green eyes sparkling – and with a jolt, Ben realized it wasn't a lad at all, but Emily! She was wearing boys' clothes and had pinned all her hair up, tucking it neatly beneath a smart corduroy cap.

Ben recognized some of the spare clothes he'd left behind in his hotel bedroom. "That's my jacket," he managed to stutter. "And my breeches! Em, you can't wear my clothes!"

"Why ever not?" Emily asked. She smiled brightly at some of the ladies over by the reception desk, who shot disapproving glances in her direction.

"Yes – why ever not, Ben?" Jack put in with a mischievous grin.

"Well. . ." Ben floundered for a moment. "It's just not *normal*."

Emily shrugged. "It's hardly a normal situation, Ben."

"I suppose not," Ben said doubtfully. "I've just never seen a girl in breeches before." Then he grinned. "But if any girl could get away with it, it's you, Emily!"

Uncle Edwin threaded his way across the lobby

towards them. His smile faded when he saw Emily, and he raised an eyebrow. "Breeches?" he queried.

"Breeches," Emily confirmed. "It's the most practical solution, Uncle Edwin. After all, we're about to embark on a dangerous mission, galloping for days across the Polish countryside. Surely you don't expect me to struggle with a dozen layers of frilly petticoat?"

Edwin laughed and shook his head. "Well, when you put it like that. . ."

"Thank you," Emily said with a smile. She glanced at Jack. "I suppose you're going to tell me now that you've arranged for me to have a side-saddle?"

"Well, yes, but that's easily changed," Jack replied with a good-natured grin.

As Emily headed determinedly for the doors, Jack nudged Ben. "Fancy Em wearing breeches," he said in an admiring voice. "I reckon Roman Cinska's goin' to have 'is hands full with her!"

By mid-afternoon they were riding hard and fast, striking a route that took them directly south-west. Branches caught at their arms and legs as the horses galloped along wooded pathways and raced across snow-dusted fields, hooves pounding. The towers and spires of Warsaw were soon out of sight, and Jack could see the empty winter landscape stretching ahead.

Brother Lubek led the way, riding at the front of the travelling party with Edwin just behind him. The young monk had replaced his sandals with knee-high leather boots and his brown robes billowed over a pair of thick woollen breeches borrowed from Ben.

Behind Brother Lubek and Edwin rode Emily, whose cheeks glowed from the brisk wind. Beside her, Ben crouched low over his horse's mane.

Jack brought up the rear on a horse that Kaspar had laughingly told him was called "Apollo". He could feel the chill wind biting through his clothes, despite his thick travelling cloak and leather gloves. He bounced uncomfortably in the saddle, unable to find Apollo's rhythm, and by sunset his whole body was aching. He'd noticed that Emily and Ben were expert on horseback. They seemed able to guide their mounts with just the lightest touch of their heels, easily negotiating deep ditches and perilous banks of snow.

"While I," Jack muttered to himself through gritted teeth, "can only cling on to Apollo's mane and pray that 'e knows what 'e's doing!"

At dusk they came across a tumbledown stone barn nestled in the corner of a field, and Edwin Sherwood called a halt for the day. Jack slipped down from his horse and stretched the knots out of his muscles.

"How's your backside?" Ben asked with a chuckle.

"Numb," Jack grumbled, but he grinned at Ben.

The two boys followed Edwin into the barn. The interior was dark and gloomy, the air heavy with the smell of cattle dung and rotten potatoes. But the travellers gathered wood and were soon warming themselves by a fire which blazed and crackled inside a circle of stones. Smoke curled up and out of the holes in the roof. As night closed in, they ate a simple meal of smoked sausage and bread, washed down with water swigged from goatskin bottles.

Somewhere a wolf howled in the darkness, and Jack exchanged an uneasy glance with Ben and Emily.

"Do not worry," Brother Lubek said reassuringly. "The wolves will not come near us while we have the fire."

"You and I can take it in turns to sit by the wood-pile and keep the flames going," Edwin Sherwood said to the young monk.

That night, Jack wrapped himself in his travelling cloak and curled on the hard ground between Ben and Emily. He was cold, his body ached, and he knew he wasn't going to sleep a wink. . .

But the next thing he knew, a firm hand was shaking him awake and he opened his eyes to daylight and birdsong. Emily's face was smiling down at him.

"Wake up, sleepy-head," she said brightly, tucking her hair back up into her cap. "How do you feel this morning?"

Jack sat up and rubbed the back of his neck. "Like someone's been kicking me," he replied with a groan. He glanced balefully at Apollo, tethered with the others at the far end of the barn – and he could have sworn that the horse returned his look of dislike.

That morning, frost feathered the hedges and clung in white patches across the fields as they made their way onwards. At the beginning of the day's travel, Jack noticed a line of peasants in the distance, trudging across the desolate landscape. But they were soon out of sight, and as the morning wore on he didn't see another living soul. *It's as though the world is empty*, Jack thought, *and we're the only living things for miles around*.

He tried to settle into his horse's rhythm, letting his body relax and sway with every hoof-beat. He'd never be a natural horseman, he knew, but by the time Edwin Sherwood called a halt at dusk on the second day, Jack was beginning to feel more comfortable. And he could have sworn Apollo was too, because when Jack gave him a nosebag full of oats that evening, the dark-eyed beast nuzzled gently at Jack's shoulder as if to say, "Thank you."

"All right, there, boy," Jack said with a grin, and patted Apollo's neck.

The travellers slept fitfully that night, huddled together beneath a clump of trees. The darkness was kept at bay by a fire built inside a makeshift circle of stones.

"I'm afraid our food stocks are getting low," Edwin said the next morning, as he broke a loaf of hard bread into five pieces. "But hopefully this is our final day of travelling. Brother Lubek says we should reach Ornak by nightfall."

"Do you think we'll get there before Roman?" Ben asked Brother Lubek.

The young monk nodded. "I think so," he said. "A stagecoach is slow and clumsy. The driver has to look out for holes in the road, and slacken the pace for sharp bends. I remember last year I went to Krakow to visit my family and the journey by coach took four days. We are much faster on horseback."

"So when we get there, we should have a day to prepare," Emily said thoughtfully.

Edwin nodded. "Yes, we'll get the lie of the land, rest and find a decent meal," he said, handing her a chunk of hard bread.

Around noon on that third day, Brother Lubek reined in and pointed out a smudge of grey on the horizon, far away to the east. "Krakow," he said simply. "My family's hometown." He shaded his eyes and stared dead ahead. "And there, in the distance, you can just make out the Tatra Mountains. . ."

Jack's heart leaped with excitement. He squinted against the pale winter sun and saw a line of snow-capped peaks far away to the south. But there was still a long way to go, and he spurred his horse on as he'd seen the others do.

Later that afternoon Jack began to make out a thick dark line nestling against the foothills of the mountains. The line seemed to extend east and west as far as he could see.

"It's the great forest of Sosnowy Las," Brother Lubek said, when Jack asked what the dark line might be. "The name is Polish for 'Pine Forest'. This forest is like a belt around the mountains – very long, but very narrow. We go through it, and on the other side, we find Ornak."

"How far to the other side?" Edwin wanted to know.

"Three, maybe four kilometres," Brother Lubek told him.

They pressed on, picking a path which led across the frozen scrubland. A frightened rabbit darted across their path, and Jack watched its white tail flash as it disappeared behind a clump of bushes. A bird screeched as it wheeled overhead. The sun began its downward slide, and Jack found himself checking for shadows every time they passed a bush, or a barren thorn tree.

They drew nearer and nearer to the forest, and Jack was soon able to make out individual trees. There were slender beeches, ashes, and gnarled old oaks, but most of them were enormous fir-trees, as tall and straight as cathedral spires, their tops white with snow. A path led between them and disappeared into the shadowy interior. Around him, the cold air seemed strangely hushed, and Jack felt a chill of foreboding.

Edwin pulled back on his reins. "I'm not sure about the wisdom of entering a dark forest this close to sunset," he said, his face shadowed by the wide brim of his hat.

Jack glanced at the sky. The clouds were touched with

the pale pink streaks of approaching sunset. *Can we make it through the forest before nightfall?* he wondered. He caught Ben's eye, and knew his friend was as wary of entering the trees as he was.

Sosnowy Las looked dense and overgrown, with little daylight filtering down to the tangled forest floor. Jack knew that, if it was dark enough, lampirs could take human-form even during the day.

"It doesn't look like we have much choice," Emily said, standing up in her stirrups and shading her eyes with one gloved hand as she scanned the deserted landscape. "The forest stretches on for ever; we can't go around it. And we certainly can't spend another night out here in the open, not in the heart of lampir territory!"

"Ornak is not far now," Brother Lubek said, glancing up to check the position of the sun. "Maybe half-an-hour away."

"Let's press on," Ben urged. "We'll keep the pace up and get to the other side as fast as we can!"

They followed the snow-dusted path into the forest, single file, and Jack felt his heart begin to beat faster. At the rear of the party, he was the last to enter the gloom of the trees, and he glanced back over his shoulder once more, just as he passed beneath the outstretched branches of the first fir.

The sky behind him was a blaze of orange now. Something flickered across Jack's vision and he blinked.

It was a bat! Its leathery wings rustled as it flitted across the sky, and he had a chilling memory of his Mexican adventures. The Mayan demon-god had taken the form of a bat. . . *But no*, Jack thought, shaking his head, *Camazotz was vanquished months ago*. Vampires had been defeated. And lampirs certainly did not take bat-form.

Jack twisted back round in his saddle and spurred his horse on, plunging into the forest. Silence closed in around him. Nothing stirred among the trees. Even Apollo's heavy hoof-beats were hushed by the thick carpet of pine needles.

The narrow track stretched ahead, pale white in the gloom. Jack could see Emily just in front of him. A lock of auburn hair had escaped from her cap and tumbled down her back. As if she could feel his eyes on her, she turned in her saddle and grinned. Jack smiled back.

The forest was murky and dark. Towering trees formed a great wall of blackness on either side of the pathway, broken here and there by shafts of greenish light. Shadows cast by overhanging branches reached out, rippling across the ground beneath the horse's hooves. Beneath him, Apollo whickered nervously and Jack murmured a comforting word.

Then one shadow, darker than the rest, flitted across the path beneath Apollo. Jack stared at it. The shadow was almost human in shape – a body, with arms and legs and a misshapen head. . .

Jack's stomach turned over as he realized that this was no ordinary shadow. It was a lampir in shadow-form. "We've got company!" he shouted to the others.

Up ahead, Edwin heard the warning and twisted round in his saddle. His face was grim and pale in the gloomy half-light as he stared at Brother Lubek. "How much further to the other side?" he demanded.

"Not much. . ." the monk replied, but he looked worried.

"Ride faster," Emily called. "We must outrun them before it gets dark enough for them to take on human-form!"

Heels down, the riders spurred their horses on. Jack saw Edwin pull out his crop and give his mount a sharp tap on the hindquarters. The beast shot forward, and the others followed, ears pricked and nostrils flaring. Jack crouched low over Apollo's neck. The forest was filled with the dull thunder of hoof-beats now, the sound echoing through the tangled trees.

Firs flashed past on either side. Branches slashed at Jack's face. Countless shadows flickered and shimmered across the pathway – more and more lampirs coming to join the first few. The lampirs moved unnaturally fast in shadow-form, easily keeping up with the galloping horses.

"We can't outrun them!" Ben yelled. "They're too fast. Our only hope is to get back out into the daylight!"

"If there's any daylight left," Jack muttered, his teeth clenched.

But the dense forest around him seemed to be getting lighter. Jack realized he could make out individual branches on the trees nearest him, whereas before they had been indistinct shapes. The forest was thinning out. . .

"We're nearly there!" Brother Lubek cried. "I can see daylight at the edge of the trees . . . and the mountains beyond!"

Jack caught a glimpse of the sky. It was dusky blue, still streaked with orange light here and there from the sunset, but nightfall wasn't far away.

And the moment darkness closed in, they would be in the utmost danger, Jack knew. Because then the lampirs would rear up in human-form and tear the party of riders apart with vicious fangs.

They burst out into the open country once more and Jack saw to his amazement that they were now in the foothills of the mountains. The land was rocky and uneven. Low, bleak hills rolled away in front of them, rising to the white-capped mountains which looked so close that Jack felt as though he only had to reach out a hand to touch them. They were shrouded in purplish light in the dusk, their deep chasms filled with shadow.

And winking in the midst of those shadows was a faraway cluster of tiny lights.

"It's Ornak!" Brother Lubek cried, pointing. "There's the village – dead ahead."

"Keep riding!" Edwin yelled, wheeling his horse

round so that he could bring up the rear. "We don't have much daylight left."

They urged their mounts onwards. But Jack could feel that Apollo was tiring. Three days of hard riding across-country had taken its toll. He leaned forward over the horse's mane, feeling the heat rise from his mount's sweating neck. "You can do it, Apollo," Jack muttered. "Come on, now. . ."

The lights ahead shone more brightly, and Jack realized with a sinking heart that darkness was closing in fast. The sun had finally dipped below the horizon and night was falling.

The first star twinkled overhead in the dusky blue sky. Something roared up ahead, filling the night air with sound. And a rippling shadow rose up abruptly on Jack's left. It snarled as it materialized into human-form, and Jack caught a fleeting glimpse of a lampir. Half-rotted skin was peeling from its face, leaving gaping holes where a nose should have been.

"Faster!" Edwin bellowed.

The lampir hurled itself forwards, reaching for Jack. But Jack jerked his reins, and Apollo veered just enough to avoid being caught.

But the first lampir was joined by another, and soon Jack could see three or four more closing in. He kicked Apollo on and the horse shot forward, leaving the lampirs behind.

Up ahead, Jack heard Brother Lubek and Ben give

startled cries. Too late, he realized his friends were reining in. Their mounts' hooves churned the half-frozen earth as they wheeled around.

Jack clung on as Apollo reared in fright, hooves pawing the air. He felt himself begin to slip backwards. . .

But Emily had seen what was happening. Quickly, she reached across from her own horse and seized Jack's bridle, hauling Apollo's head back down.

Jack fell forward into his saddle. "Thanks, Em," he managed to say.

The horses pranced and snorted, grinding their bits between their teeth.

"What is it?" Emily yelled at Ben and Brother Lubek. "We were outstripping the lampirs. Why have you stopped?"

But looking past them, Jack could see all too well. A fast-flowing river cut right across their path. Gleaming black rocks glittered beneath the surface. Jack realized he'd been able to hear the roaring torrent for some time, but his panicking brain hadn't identified the sound as water.

But there was no time to think; the lampirs were catching up. The nearest of the creatures snatched at Emily's foot. With a yell, Jack kicked the lampir away. He felt his foot connect with desiccated flesh and dusty bone. The lampir staggered back, snarling at Jack.

"This way," Brother Lubek shouted, turning his mount to the right. "There's a ford!"

Jack urged Apollo on and the horse flew forwards. The lampir howled with fury as it realized its prey was getting away. Glancing back, Jack saw it transform into shadow-form, then ripple swiftly across the ground in pursuit.

Edwin was cursing as he slashed his crop at another lampir that had come too close. And Emily was half-standing in her stirrups, her knees bent and her weight flung forward over her horse's neck as she desperately urged her mount to go faster. She'd lost her cap, so her hair now hung loose down her back, spiky with pine needles.

Up ahead, Ben gave a triumphant shout. "The ford!" he yelled. "I can see the wooden markers sticking out of the water! They're showing us where it's shallow enough to cross!"

But Jack could see something else. . .

The approach to the ford was blocked.

Up ahead, a hundred snarling lampirs had gathered across the pathway. Grey river-mist curled around their feet. Somewhere a wolf howled, and a bat dived to flit low across the surface of the water.

And Jack saw, with a sickening certainty, that there was no way past the lampirs. . .

They were trapped.

CHAPTER SIX

Emily stared in horror at the slathering battalion up ahead. There was nowhere to go. Lampirs blocked the way forwards, and a glance over her shoulder showed that they were fast closing in behind.

The only way out of this situation is to go through *them*, she thought, clenching her teeth. "Don't stop!" she yelled to the others as loudly as she could. "Brace yourselves and just *ride*!"

She spurred her horse on, dimly aware of Ben and Brother Lubek on one side of her and Jack on the other. They were all standing up in their stirrups now, their faces blank masks of single-minded determination.

The horses crashed through the host of lampirs. Emily felt a sickening thud as one of the creatures was trampled beneath her mount's thundering hooves, and then suddenly she was knee-deep in the river. The freezing water made her gasp as it swirled around her legs. She could feel the current trying to drag her downstream.

Quickly, she pulled on the reins and corrected her course, her gaze fixed on the far bank which, thankfully, seemed to be clear of lampirs. She could see a stony path, wreathed in mist, which led away from the ford. Beyond it, the land rose towards the cluster of lights which signalled the village of Ornak.

The town looked small and compact, a ring of dark houses set around a tall stone cross. The sound of raised voices and dogs barking carried to Emily's ears on the clear, chill night air. Now she could see more lights chasing back the night. Lanterns bobbed in the darkness as people dashed this way and that.

Abruptly, Emily realized that some of the villagers were carrying flaming torches. Relief washed over her at the sight of the flames – they would be safe here, at last. Emily urged her horse up out of the river and on towards the village, closely followed by Brother Lubek, Jack and Ben, with Edwin bringing up the rear.

Ahead of her, a man dressed in a rough sheepskin coat and fur hat stood on the outskirts of the village. He bellowed something and bent to touch his torch to the ground. Instantly a wall of flame leaped upwards and he fell back.

Emily saw to her horror that the man had set fire to the ground. All around one side of the village, a sheet of bright orange flames, a metre and a half tall, had begun to spring up.

With a jolt, Emily realized that the villagers had filled

a ditch with some kind of flammable liquid – tar, maybe, or oil. It rippled blackly as the fire raced around the eastern-most reaches of the village and took hold.

She guided her horse to the right. The western edges of the village were still in darkness. If they could make it that far, there was no fire there. But even as she approached, a group of men with torches ran forwards and the western-most reaches of the village leaped into flame.

Emily could see that soon the two walls of fire would meet, effectively barring any way into the village.

Ben drew up alongside Emily and his horrified gaze met hers. "We have to make it into the village," he cried urgently. "Come on, Em, before it closes us out!" and he spurred his mount on towards the remaining gap in the fiery wall.

Brother Lubek was right behind him, followed closely by Edwin. Emily was about to follow, when she saw that Jack was struggling with his horse. Poor Apollo was baulking at the sight of the flames. He pawed the ground and skittered backwards with a snort, rolling his eyes until the whites showed. Foam flecked his mouth and bridle.

Emily saw Jack's face, chalky-pale in the darkness, and behind him she saw a score of lampirs.

"Hold on, Jack!" Emily yelled as she galloped back towards her friend. She rode past Apollo, then turned and came up on him from behind. As she passed, she raised her crop and brought it down sharply on Apollo's hindquarters.

With an outraged whinny, the terrified horse bolted forwards through the gap in the flames, carrying Jack to safety. And Emily wasn't far behind. With the lampirs closing in, she kicked her horse on and her mare obediently flew towards the fiery wall. The gap was now so small that Emily felt the heat on her face as she rode through.

One lampir made a grab for her as the mare leaped through the flames. Emily felt its claw-like hand graze the back of her jacket. But the gap in the wall of fire finally closed behind her, and the lampir was trapped. It caught light, burning and twisting in a blaze of orange flames until nothing was left but ash.

Behind her, beyond the wall of fire that now completely surrounded the village, Emily could see the hulking shapes of the lampirs pacing up and down. But there was nothing the creatures could do to penetrate the flames. The friends were safe.

Emily brought her horse to a halt and turned to look at Ben, Jack, Edwin and Brother Lubek. Their faces were streaked with sweat and they looked exhausted, but they all grinned at her.

Emily grinned back, feeling weak with relief. They had arrived in Ornak.

CHAPTER SEVEN

Jack's heart pounded. He had escaped the lampirs, only to see a group of about twenty men lunging forwards to surround the travellers, and seize the reins of the horses. Dressed in woollen jackets, baggy trousers and fur hats, the men were all armed with axes and long-handled scythes. Several of them held flaming torches which they jabbed upwards, perilously close to the riders' faces.

"They ain't lookin' friendly," Jack muttered.

"Speak to them, Brother Lubek," Edwin urged. "Tell them we mean them no harm."

But before Brother Lubek could say a word, the villagers began to pull him down from his horse. They patted at his monk's robes, and exclaimed in tones of wonder when someone pulled back the young monk's woollen hood to reveal his tonsured head.

A toothless old man began gabbling excitedly. He patted at the wooden cross hanging around Brother

Lubek's neck on a knotted cord, and Jack caught the word "*mnich*" which he'd heard before at the monastery. He thought it meant *monk*.

Another man stepped forwards and sternly waved the others away from Brother Lubek. He was in his mid-forties, small but strongly-muscled beneath his thick sheepskin coat, with a large black moustache that drooped either side of his firm mouth. His dark eyes glittered in the firelight as he barked questions at Brother Lubek.

"*Nie jestesmy wampirami,*" Lubek said to the man. "I am telling him that we are not lampirs," he added, glancing up at Edwin, who was still on horseback beside him.

"Well done, Brother Lubek," Edwin said, looking relieved.

The dark-eyed man with the black moustache had been following their exchange. "E-English. . .?" he interrupted, frowning fiercely in Edwin's direction. "You are English?"

"Yes," Edwin said. "We've come from London."

At that, the man's stern face broke into a beaming smile. "I speak the English," he said proudly. "*Nauczylem sie nagielskiego od profesora uniwerystetu wiele lat temu.*"

Brother Lubek quickly translated his words. "He says he learned from a professor at university, many years ago," the young monk explained.

62

The man slapped his own chest and declared, "I am name of Pavel."

As Pavel continued in lilting Polish, Brother Lubek translated. "He says . . . this is his village. He welcomes us."

"Tell Pavel we're very pleased to meet him," Edwin said. "And we're grateful for his kind welcome."

As the three friends and Edwin slipped down from their horses, a few of the villagers began to push closer curiously. But others hung back, evidently still uneasy.

The head villager spoke again and Brother Lubek nodded.

"Pavel says we should accompany him to his house," the young monk said. "He wishes us to eat with his family."

Jack hesitated, stroking Apollo's nose with his hand. "What about the horses?" he asked.

"Yes," Emily put in. "Is there somewhere we can give them food and water, first?"

At a word from Pavel, a few boys darted forwards eagerly and led the shivering horses away to be fed and watered. Meanwhile, two young women with gold hoop earrings pressed close to Emily, gazing at her breeches and fingering her long hair in fascination, as if they weren't sure whether she was a boy or a girl.

Jack caught a few of the elders staring at him curiously. Eventually one of them, an old woman with a bright green headscarf and a black woollen shawl, pushed her way to the front of the crowd, peering closely at Jack.

With a chuckle, she reached out a gnarled hand and patted his cheek as she chattered away to him in Polish.

"Er, pardon?" Jack said, smiling at the old woman and shooting an uncertain look at Brother Lubek, in hopes of a translation.

"She thinks you're Polish," the young monk explained. "Her name is Roza. And she says she knows your face."

Jack grinned. "That ain't the first time someone Polish has thought they recognized me," he declared.

"That's right. Filip Cinska thought you were Polish, too," Emily said thoughtfully. "Remember when we first met him, in London? He spoke to you in Polish and was amazed when you didn't understand."

"I remember," Jack said. "But Filip made a mistake. A Londoner through and through, that's me!"

Even as he spoke, a tiny doubt crept into the back of Jack's mind. He was an orphan, after all. So could he really be sure that he didn't have Polish blood flowing through his veins?

But there wasn't time to think about that now, because Pavel was barking orders at the village men, sending them hurrying off in all directions.

"They are forming a watch," Brother Lubek said, in answer to Edwin's enquiring look. "Pavel has ordered twenty men to stand guard all night and keep the fires burning. But now he is saying we should all follow him."

"Come!" Pavel said, nodding and waving the newcomers on into the village square.

"He says we are obviously in need of food and shelter," Brother Lubek translated. "We are to go to his house . . . and eat like kings!"

Pavel's house had a tall, pointed roof and pretty blue and orange shutters. Once inside, the friends gratefully sat down on chunky wooden chairs, while Pavel's wife, who Brother Lubek said was called Yelena, bustled around handing out wooden bowls into which she ladled *krupnik*, a chunky beef stew generously laced with herbs and barley.

Ben cupped his hands around his bowl, warming his fingers. The men and women of the village were ranged around the room, some sitting on chairs and tables, casting interested looks at the travellers. Others leaned against the walls with their arms folded, chattering quietly. Some of them were wary of the newcomers, and kept their distance, but several caught Ben's eye and smiled in a friendly way.

A slender woman with a pretty face moved gracefully around the room, handing out bread from a wicker basket. A little boy, about six years old, with enormous brown eyes, clung to her colourful, embroidered skirts as if worried he might lose her in the crush.

But when they came to Ben, the little boy grinned and sat down, resting his bony little body against Ben's leg. The slender woman – who was obviously the boy's mother – smiled as she offered Ben some bread.

Ben helped himself to a roll and then turned to the boy. "Ben," he said, tapping his own chest with one hand. "My name is Ben."

The little boy's face lit up. "Florian," he said, mimicking Ben's gesture and patting himself squarely on the chest.

They grinned at each other, instant friends.

Nearby, settled in front of the cosy fire which roared in the stone fireplace, Edwin and Pavel were talking. Although Pavel had a basic command of English, Ben saw that Edwin was relying on Brother Lubek to translate parts of their conversation.

"It's amazing how many people can fit into one room," the archaeologist chuckled, looking round. "There must be more than thirty villagers in here!"

"The heat of so many packed bodies keeps us warm in the winter," Pavel joked. "But seriously, they all want to have a look at you! Usually the only outsider to come through here is the pedlar, Antoni. He comes once a month with his wagon, bringing us fresh supplies of tar and oil to keep our ditches burning."

"Why do you stay here?" Emily asked. "It's so dangerous."

"It is our home," Pavel said simply. "We have always lived here – and we refuse to be chased out by lampirs! Besides. . ." he shrugged, "now we have learned to fight them. And they do not always strike Ornak, you know. There are other villages."

The old woman in the bright green headscarf, Roza, lowered herself into an armchair by the fire and muttered something. Pavel nodded, smoothing his heavy black moustache with his thumb.

"Roza has just reminded me that people *do* sometimes leave," he said. "But not many. And not often. The last couple left many years ago." He frowned for a moment, as if trying to remember. "Stefan Kowalski and his heavily-pregnant wife. They had lost their two eldest children in a lampir raid. . ."

Pavel looked sombre for a moment. "That was in the days before we knew how to fight back," he said. "We suffered then. The lampirs would come at night to snatch our children. The Kowalskis could not face losing another infant, so they decided to leave Ornak for ever. Yes – people leave." He shrugged philosophically. "But also, people come. The road to Ornak has been busy this week! We had another stranger arrive yesterday, you know! A tall man, very tall." Pavel nodded in Edwin's direction. "Taller even than you, Englishman. He too came from Warsaw."

Across the room, someone muttered, "Doktor . . . doktor. . ."

Ben's heart began to beat faster. A tall man from Warsaw, who called himself doctor?

It sounded as though Roman Cinska had beaten them to Ornak after all.

CHAPTER EIGHT

Emily's heart thumped hard and she set down her soup spoon. She turned to Ben and Jack. "It must be Roman," she said softly.

"It certainly sounds like it," Ben said grimly. "Although we thought we'd get here before him. Brother Lubek thought the journey by stagecoach would probably take four days."

"Indeed I did," Brother Lubek put in, looking anxious. "But perhaps Roman was able to travel faster. After all, he was alone, he could have thrown out the luggage, and there would have been no stops to let passengers on and off."

"He could have kept going, day and night," Emily said.

"If the poor horses survived," Jack muttered, twisting the gold ring on his middle finger.

"So what do we do now?" Ben asked.

"First we need to find out exactly where Roman

Cinska is and what he wants," Edwin said. "Then we can formulate a plan."

"The doctor is a friend of yours?" Pavel asked, glancing curiously at Edwin Sherwood.

"He's nobody's friend," Ben muttered darkly. "Least of all ours."

"But we *have* come here to look for him," Edwin told Pavel. "Do you know where he is?"

Pavel spoke quickly in Polish to a few of the other villagers. A couple of the men shook their heads and shrugged.

"They say they did not pay much attention to him," Brother Lubek said, translating. "They think he was simply passing through Ornak on his way to somewhere else. Nobody has seen him since he arrived earlier today."

"You'd better tell them what we know about Roman Cinska, Brother Lubek," Edwin said heavily. "They need to be warned."

"And they might be able to help us work out exactly why he's come to Ornak," Emily added thoughtfully.

Brother Lubek nodded and sat forward with his elbows on his knees, talking in Polish to Pavel and the other villagers. The room was so quiet that all Emily could hear above the young monk's voice was the crackle and pop of coals in the hearth. It seemed as though the whole room held its breath, while Brother Lubek explained that the stranger who had arrived earlier that day had been a new and more powerful form of lampir.

"The tall doktor is a lampir?" Pavel said, his face white with shock.

"Half-lampir, half-human," Edwin corrected, and Brother Lubek translated for the benefit of the villagers. "Roman Cinska is different to ordinary lampirs because he can take human-form even in daylight. And he commands the undead to do his bidding. In Warsaw he created an army – a legion of lampirs determined to destroy the city."

At this news, the villagers all began to mutter among themselves. Across the room, old Roza sat down heavily on the nearest empty chair.

"*Zgubieni!*" someone cried. "*Jestesmy wszyscy przeznaczeni!*"

"They're saying they're doomed," Brother Lubek said, looking worried. "They feel that all is lost now that a powerful half-lampir like Roman has come to Ornak. They are shocked that they didn't see him for what he was."

"Lampir . . . lampir. . ." the word spread across the room in a hundred frantic whispers. Emily thought that even the walls of Pavel's little house seemed to quiver with fear. An old woman began to tear at her own clothes, wailing.

Emily stood up, anxious to calm things down. "You're not alone in this fight," she said firmly and loudly, signalling for Brother Lubek to translate. "We can help

71

you, because we've done battle with hundreds, maybe even thousands, of lampirs over the past few weeks. We defeated them in London, and in Warsaw, and we intend to defeat them here too."

Emily was gratified to see that her words were having an effect. A calmness seemed to fall over the room. And someone escorted the wailing woman outside.

"We're going to fight," Emily continued in a level voice. "And we're going to win! But we need your help."

Pavel spread his hands wide. "Anything," he said gruffly. "Just ask."

"First, we need to know why Roman Cinska has come here," Emily said, sitting down again. "We know that Ornak was the birthplace of lampirism, and that Count Casimir Lampirska ruled here. . ." As she uttered the name Lampirska, Emily saw a dozen people cower and cross themselves fearfully.

"Seems Count Casimir still has a powerful hold here," Jack muttered.

"I thought he'd been defeated by dhampirs," Ben put in, frowning thoughtfully.

"He *was* defeated," Pavel said firmly. "Many years ago, Count Casimir Lampirska was sealed in his grave by dhampirs." He glanced at the friends. "You have heard of dhampirs before?"

Emily's mind immediately flew to the Dhampir Tome with its cracked and yellowing pages full of ancient legends and myths. She had spent hours poring over it,

72

translating it into English with Filip Cinska. And one compelling tale had surfaced again and again – that of the dhampirs, a line of Polish families who had grown immune to the lampir plague. For centuries they had fought and defeated many of the creatures. It was said that lampirs had grown to fear these extraordinary men and women, shying away from the power of the dhampir.

"We've read about them," Emily said. "We know that they were very powerful."

Old Roza leaned forwards. "Did you know that dhampir blood was one of the few weapons we had against the lampir?" she asked, her words quickly translated by Brother Lubek. "It was sheer poison. A single drop of dhampir blood spilled on a lampir's flesh could turn the creature to ash more quickly than fire!"

"Yes, I remember reading about that in the Dhampir Tome," Emily said. "But our friend Filip Cinska told us that there are no dhampirs left. The last dhampir died many years ago. Isn't that right?"

"Indeed, there are no more dhampirs here," Pavel acknowledged heavily. "For many years dhampirs battled against the lampir plague," he explained, "and it was they who were instrumental in the forging of the great bells. Dhampir Bells they were called. There were twelve of them in all."

"Twelve?" Jack raised his eyebrows.

Pavel nodded. "Seven were forged by one particular dhampir family, who used the bells to strike a fatal blow to Count Casimir and his barons. Five more bells were created by other dhampir families across Poland. These were to be used against other lampirs as the need arose. To my knowledge, only one of the five bells remains in existence. Legend has it that this bell is kept in a monastery in Warsaw."

The friends and Brother Lubek exchanged keen glances.

"The legend was right," Ben told Pavel. "The bell was kept in the Monastery of St Wenceslaus, where Brother Lubek lives."

Pavel's face brightened. "This is marvellous news!" he said excitedly.

But Jack shook his head. "The bell ain't there any more," he said.

The head villager looked at the three friends, obviously mystified. "Then . . . where is it?" he asked.

Emily took a deep breath. "Shortly before Christmas, the Dhampir Bell was taken from the monastery and brought to England," she explained. "With Filip Cinska's help, we were able to use it to lure the lampirs of London to their doom. Then we brought it back to Poland, and used it to defeat the Warsaw lampirs, too."

"Then you have seen its power," Pavel said eagerly. "And harnessed it for yourselves? Few people in this world have been so fortunate!"

A few of the villagers murmured amongst themselves and looked at the party of travellers with new respect.

"Yes, but then we had to destroy the bell. So that it could not be used to reawaken the lampirs in Warsaw," Jack explained. "And the Dhampir Tome said that most of the other bells have also been lost or destroyed," he finished.

"Lost. . . ?" Pavel raised his heavy black eyebrows. "Is that what they are saying?" He shrugged. "I suppose 'lost' is as good a word as any. The bells have served their purpose. It is probably better if the world believes them to be lost."

Emily glanced at Ben, Jack and Edwin. "What do you mean?" she asked curiously. "Are you saying that the other Dhampir Bells *aren't* lost after all?" She felt a ripple of excitement. "Do you know where they are, Pavel?"

"Of course," Pavel said simply. "Seven of them are here in Ornak."

"*Here?*" Emily repeated in amazement.

The friends exchanged a stunned look.

Emily's mind was racing. "So that's why Roman Cinska has come!" she exclaimed. "He has come in search of the other bells!"

"He wants to harness a bit of power for himself," Jack put in.

"Where are these seven bells?" Edwin asked quietly.

"Do not worry," Pavel said reassuringly. "They are beyond the reach of any man."

"But we're not dealing with just a man," Emily said

starkly. "We're dealing with a half-lampir, half-human hybrid."

Pavel blushed and nodded. "Of course," he said. "You must forgive me. This idea of a half-man and half-lampir is new to me." He put his head in his hands for a moment. "I wish that we had known," he said, his voice muffled. "We would have stopped him. He has had many hours to do his evil work, but none of us were aware of it, for no one goes near the place now."

"What evil work?" Emily asked.

Taking a deep breath, the head villager straightened up and gazed hopelessly at the newcomers. "Seven Dhampir Bells were used to defeat Count Casimir Lampirska and his six barons," he said. "One bell for Count Lampirska, and one for each of the barons. The count and his lampir-barons were mesmerized by the sound of the bells. When the bells were rung, they could not resist. They were entranced!"

"Just like the lampirs in London," Ben put in.

"A lampir will follow that sound to the ends of the earth," Pavel said. "And so it was with the count. The dhampirs lured him to the old church that stands outside the village, and down into his family's crypt. And there the count and his barons were walled up. Brick by brick they were sealed into the very fabric of the burial chamber beneath the church!" He sighed, and rubbed a hand over his chin. "And the lampir-count and his men are imprisoned there still, in an eternal sleep, held by a special incantation which prevents them from waking."

"And what happened to the seven bells?" Ben queried.

"They were also sealed into the walls of the tomb," Pavel said. "For if those bells are ever rung again, they will awaken the count and his barons. So, you see, if Roman Cinska breaks through the wall and retrieves the bells, then he may use them to release Count Lampirska and his barons. If that happens, seven dark devils that none of us can fight will once again be free to walk the earth! That is the evil work that your Roman could be doing – even as we speak. He may be releasing the Seven!"

All around the room, hands flashed as dozens of villagers crossed themselves.

"If that's the case, then we have to stop him now," Emily said firmly.

Jack and Ben nodded grimly.

"We'll need weapons," Edwin said, standing up. "And torches. We can't go out there without fire and flame."

"You can't go out there at all!" Pavel exclaimed in horror. "The old church is outside the ring of fire that surrounds the village! It would be madness to venture out there in the dead of night."

"He's right," Brother Lubek said. "It wouldn't be just Roman Cinska we'd have to fight, but all those lampirs too!"

There was a moment of stillness in the room. The

villagers stared from Pavel to the newcomers, some of them not able to understand the rapid exchange which had just taken place. Others trembled and kissed their crucifixes, their eyes dark with fear.

After a moment, old Roza spoke up, and Brother Lubek translated. "She says we must wait until daylight. There will be no lampirs then, just Roman Cinska – and you will have more chance of defeating him if he is your only foe."

"Perhaps she's right," Edwin Sherwood admitted.

"But by morning Roman might have released the bells!" protested Emily.

"But not necessarily the count and the barons," Pavel said. "He will not know the incantation required to release the dark devils from their captivity. It will take him time to decipher the inscriptions which have been carved across their tombs—"

"Inscriptions?" interrupted Edwin, looking interested. "Why has the incantation been inscribed on the tombs?"

"It was put there as a warning," Pavel explained. "So that no one would make the mistake of releasing the count accidentally. Indeed, there is a wealth of lampir-legend inscribed upon the walls of the crypt, all of it written by dhampirs who wished to pass on their knowledge to future generations."

"Know your enemy," Ben muttered with a nod.

"In what language are these inscriptions written?" Edwin asked.

"The words are strange and complicated," the head villager replied, shaking his head. "I think it is some kind of medieval Polish mixed with Latin."

"Just like in the Dhampir Tome," Emily said, recalling the long hours she had spent poring over the pages with Filip Cinska.

"I think the very nature of that complicated script should buy us a few hours," Edwin said. "We will go in the morning. In the meantime, we should gather weapons and torches – and get some sleep if we can."

Several of the villagers spoke eagerly, including old Roza and the slender woman who had passed around the bread basket. Brother Lubek translated their words.

"These kind people wish to show their gratitude by offering us their spare bedrooms," the young monk said.

"I must admit," Jack said slowly. "I wouldn't mind having a bit of sleep before I have to face Roman in the morning!"

"You're right," Emily agreed. "Let's meet at daybreak. Then we can finish Roman Cinska before he has a chance to release the count and his barons: the Seven!"

CHAPTER NINE

Ben slept better than he had expected. He was woken at first light by Daria, the slender woman who was Florian's mother. She made him a breakfast of sweet, creamy porridge and Ben sat at her kitchen table to eat it, under the watchful gaze of Florian himself.

"Ben!" Florian said emphatically, in between spoonfuls of his own porridge.

"Florian!" Ben replied, and they both grinned at each other, knowing that despite the barrier of language, a firm friendship had somehow been made.

After he'd eaten, Ben made his way outside into the square with Florian at his heels. They found Jack and Emily sorting through a pile of wooden torches. Each torch was made from a one-metre length of wood, one end padded in cotton wadding which had been soaked in tar, the other end bound with rope to make a hand-grip.

Ben noticed that Emily was wearing her breeches again. She shot him a determined look as he joined them, as if she was daring him to make a comment. Ben just grinned.

The sky was grey and overcast, and the air was sharp with the tang of smoke and burnt oil from last night's defences. Although it was early, there were a few villagers up and about, most of them tired-looking men of the watch, trudging back to their beds. One or two of them glanced curiously at the newcomers.

Pavel and Brother Lubek were talking quietly to Edwin, when Ben, Jack and Emily finished assembling the torches and came over to join them. Edwin was sharpening an already lethal-looking knife on a piece of whetstone. The blade glittered as the archaeologist sheathed it and shoved it into his belt. "We'll use flame as our first resort," he said. "The plan is to trap Roman in the underground crypt and set fire to him there."

Edwin opened his canvas knapsack and revealed a collection of small earthenware jars, each one wrapped in a strip of cloth to stop them rattling. "Roza and I made these last night," he explained. "They're grenades. Each one is full of oil. You throw it as hard as you can at the ground, and when the jar smashes, the oil spills. We simply touch our torches to the oil to start a blaze that will engulf Roman Cinska and finish him for ever."

Jack handed round the wooden torches. Ben sent little Florian home, and the group made their way out of the square and along the village's main street. Several people appeared at the windows to watch them pass. Some of them came running out with crucifixes which they pressed into the travellers' hands. Others, like Roza, and Florian's mother, Daria, held up two crossed fingers for luck.

They were just nearing the outskirts of the village when Jack suddenly gave Ben a sharp nudge. "Just take a look at *that*!" he muttered.

Ben looked where his friend was pointing and shivered. An enormous ruined castle stood at the top of a craggy rockface, high in the mountains above the village. Its broken battlements and turrets towered up against the early-morning sky. It was an impressive and ominous sight.

"That is Castle Lampirska," Pavel said quietly. "And there ahead is the old church."

Set against the backdrop of the majestic mountains was a squat building with a black slate roof and a tall bell-tower. The windswept graveyard which surrounded it looked lonely and desolate. It was full of tumbledown tombstones and rusted iron crosses, overgrown by thorn bushes that had broken through the jagged iron railings surrounding the cemetery.

"Nobody goes there now," Pavel explained. "My people are afraid, because of Count Lampirska. These days we worship in a small wooden church just off the village square."

Together they crossed the ditch which surrounded the village. It was still smouldering in parts, and the sides were slick with oil.

"Inside the church you will find the Lampirska family's tomb," Pavel said, and Ben could hear a tremor of fear in his voice. "It is a huge black marble monument which forms the entrance to the crypt. There is a door, and some stairs which lead underground."

"You've been very helpful, Pavel," Edwin said, shaking the head villager's hand. "Stay here and keep watch for our return."

Pavel wished them luck, then he stood and watched as the little party made its way across the wide expanse of barren scrubland between the village and the church.

Ben couldn't resist another glance at the ruined castle. A lone bat wheeled around one of the turrets, a splash of black against the pale morning sky.

Jack had obviously spotted the bat too, because he turned to Ben and murmured, "Makes you think o' Camazotz, don't it?"

Ben nodded, wondering suddenly whether Roman Cinska would prove as powerful as the Mayan demon-god.

"I can't see any sign of Roman out here," Jack said, a short time later. "He must be inside the church." He was walking just ahead of the others, his boots crunching the snowy gravel of the graveyard.

"You'd think there would be tracks to follow," Emily murmured, staring at the ground. "Footprints in the snow. . ."

"Not if he used shadow-form," Jack reminded her.

"Looks like someone's been through here recently," Ben called. He was over by the entrance to the church, where a set of half-rotten timber doors hung askew on rusted hinges. "The snow's been disturbed where the doors have been pushed open."

Jack hurried over to peer into the shadowy interior of the church. Dark wooden pews stood in rows on either side of a central aisle, and there was a stained-glass window halfway down one wall, letting in the faintest glimmer of cold daylight.

"It's dark in there," Jack said to the others. "We're going to need light."

Edwin fished his tinder box out of his pocket, and carefully lit the tar-soaked cotton wrapped around the head of his torch. Then he touched the flame to Jack's, Emily's, Ben's and Brother Lubek's in turn. The torches flared and flickered in the grey morning light, and Jack could feel the sudden warmth on his cheeks.

Together, they stepped inside the church. As they advanced down the aisle, the flickering light from their torches sent weird shadows dancing across the walls, but it was clear that there was nobody else in the church. Their hushed footsteps were the only sound.

Jack held his torch up high, throwing light on to the church walls where faded frescoes leaped into glorious colour. Dull gold halos gleamed around the heads of painted angels on the vaulted ceiling, and dusty oak wood panels glowed softly. There was an altar draped in the rotten remnants of a red and gold altar cloth at the far end of the church. And beside the altar, shrouded in shadow, was an enormous black stone tomb, just as Pavel had described.

The tomb was taller than a man and three times as wide. It was a solid rectangular block of black stone, intricately carved with coats-of-arms, swags of foliage, and scrolls. On it reclined an effigy of a stern-faced man with his hands folded across his chest. His long robes and armoured breastplate were so skilfully carved that they looked real. The whole monument was thick with dust.

"Grim-lookin' fellow, that," Jack muttered, moving closer and peering at the effigy. "Wonder who 'e was?"

"Probably the first Count Lampirska," Edwin said, his archaeologist's eye assessing the lines of the spiral columns. "I'd say this dates from the early-medieval period, which would fit in nicely with the history of the Lampirska family." He reached up and gently wiped some of the dust from the effigy's robes. "It's a beautiful tomb, isn't it?"

"Beautiful," Emily agreed. "But somehow horrible as well. It's so . . . so. . ." she hesitated, searching for the right word.

"So *black*?" Jack finished for her. And Emily grinned and nodded.

Ben ran a finger over an inscription carved into the

side of the tomb. "What does this say, Brother Lubek?" he asked.

The young monk held his torch closer, and the flickering flames turned the gold lettering of the inscription to molten fire.

"'Beneath this monument . . . lie the mortal remains . . . of seven generations of the great Lampirska family and their servants,'" Brother Lubek translated slowly. "'This place is sacred to the memory of all those who pass beneath its arches on their journey to the glorious afterlife.'"

Jack snorted at that. "Count Casimir obviously decided that the afterlife wasn't glorious enough for him!" he muttered. "Him and his barons had other plans."

"Luckily for the villagers of Ornak, the dhampirs were able to thwart those plans," Edwin said grimly. He shrugged off his knapsack and handed each of them a little grenade jar. "And we're here to make sure that Roman Cinska doesn't change all that!"

A narrow, pointed archway inlaid with gold had been set into one end of the tomb, and Jack could just make out the top of a flight of stairs leading down into the darkness below.

"This must be the entrance to the crypt," he said. "Roman ain't up here, so it stands to reason 'e's probably down there!"

Ben gave him a taut nod. "Let's go," he said.

The steps down into the underground crypt were so narrow the friends had to make their way down in single file. Their torches guttered against the low ceiling, and Jack was aware of the smell of charred wood and soot . . . and something else. Something dry and musty. The smell of death.

The crypt was a series of vaulted chambers, one leading off the other. The flickering light from the five torches chased back the shadows, and in the first chamber Jack could see archways and niches crammed with white stone.

But when he looked more closely, he saw that it *wasn't* stone. Jack's stomach turned over as he realized that the niches were actually stacked high with *bones*! Skulls stared out at him, empty eyed. He glanced upwards and saw a gruesome chandelier, fashioned entirely from tiny finger-bones. Glowing ghostly-white in the semi-darkness, the chandelier hung from a central point on the arched ceiling.

Above the entrance to the next chamber was a coat of arms, also made entirely of bones. *Probably arm-bones, by the looks of them*, Jack thought grimly. "Brings a whole new meaning to the words 'coat of arms'," he whispered to Ben.

"This is an ossuary," Edwin said softly, his voice tinged with wonder. "A bone-house. . ."

"Blimey. . ." Jack muttered. "Give me a good old-fashioned graveyard any day."

They made their way through the low archway, beneath the coat of arms, into the second chamber. It was larger than the first and here the walls were lined with black marble ledges, like bookshelves. But instead of books, the ledges held caskets draped with lengths of half-rotten silk and velvet – the coffins of the Lampirska family!

"If that's the Lampirskas," muttered Jack, "then who were that lot back there in the bone-house?"

"Servants," Edwin told him. "All the family's old retainers would have been laid to rest alongside their masters."

"There's nowhere for Roman to hide in here," Emily whispered. "He must be further on, in the next chamber."

"Let's take him by surprise," Edwin murmured, his voice barely audible.

They advanced slowly and silently, walking on tiptoe. . .

But Jack was shocked to realize that the third chamber was empty too.

This chamber was a large, eight-sided vault with a high curved ceiling in much the same fashion as the previous chambers. However, large portions of the walls here had been bricked and plastered. The rough red clay surface was at odds with the smooth black stone of the rest of the chamber.

The plaster on seven walls of the octagonal chamber

was intact, but Jack saw immediately that the plaster and brickwork of the eighth wall been smashed to oblivion. Rubble was strewn across the floor and a gaping hole in the wall showed an empty space lined with shelves.

Emily darted forwards. "The bells must have been sealed up behind the wall here," she said breathlessly. "Look – you can see the marks in the dust on these shelves. Seven circles – seven bells."

"But they're gone!" Ben exclaimed in frustration. "Roman's beaten us to it. He's got the Dhampir Bells!"

The friends exchanged horrified glances. Brother Lubek held his torch up high and examined the remaining seven walls of the eight-sided room. Flickering shadows danced across their roughly-plastered surfaces, and the red clay glowed like blood.

"He may have the bells," the young monk said flatly. "But obviously Roman has not yet released Count Casimir and his barons, because these other walls are still intact. . ."

Frowning, Edwin Sherwood ran his finger across several lines of inscription that had been carved into the crimson plaster. "This must be the warning that Pavel told us about," he murmured. "It's old Polish. *Very* old. Medieval, I would say. But some of the writing is Latin."

"Just like the Dhampir Tome," Emily put in. "That was written in a mixture of Old Polish and Latin."

"Can you understand what the inscription says, Em?" Ben asked.

Jack watched as Emily moved closer to Edwin, holding her torch up to light the words. She studied the writing carefully, her lips moving as she tried to decipher the ancient languages.

There was silence for a moment, broken only by the popping and crackling of the flames.

"I wish I had some of Filip's books here with me," Emily murmured eventually. "I don't recognize all these words."

"I may be able to assist with some of them," Brother Lubek said helpfully.

"Thank you," Emily replied with a grateful smile. She hesitated, and then translated a few words for them, running her finger across the intricately-carved lettering of the inscription. "'Seven bells . . . for seven arch-lampirs . . . one of whom is from the great house of Lampirska. . .'" she read. Then she paused, frowning.

With Brother Lubek's help and some assistance from Edwin on the Latin phrases, Emily managed to decipher several more lines. "'He who brings the house into illness. . .' No, not 'illness' . . . 'disrepute'. 'He who brings the house into disrepute shall lie for ever between life and death, neither in one nor the other. . . And the only thing to raise him shall be the ringing of the seven bells from the church tower. . .'"

Without warning, an echoing boom rolled over them in a wave of sound which filled every corner of the underground chamber. Another followed it, lighter this timc, a high, sweet, fluid sound which harmonized with the first . . . and then another joined it . . . and yet another, in a ringing waterfall of melody.

The sound was magical, almost mesmerizing. A siren song which seemed to reach deep into a person's soul. The friends all gazed up at the ceiling.

"The chime of the seven bells!" Brother Lubek exclaimed suddenly in alarm.

"We're too late!" Jack cried. "Roman has rehung the seven bells in the church tower. He's trying to release the count!"

Emily suddenly backed away from the red clay wall, almost tripping in her haste. "I think he's succeeded," she muttered darkly. "Look at that!"

Everyone looked. At first Jack couldn't see what Emily meant. Surely if the count was released, then the red clay walls would disintegrate as the arch-lampirs smashed their way out? But nothing was happening to the walls. . .

Or was it?

Jack blinked and stared at the inscription. Yes, something *was* happening! Cracks had begun to appear in the red plaster. Fine lines chased each other quickly across the surface.

And then Jack noticed something else: a faint plume of charcoal-grey was seeping through the cracks in the wall. Black shadows, like wisps of smoke, were trickling from behind the inscription!

Jack glanced at the next wall and then the next, his gaze darting around the octagonal chamber.

Slowly but surely, each wall was being obscured by dense, velvety-black shadow. Count Casimir Lampirska and his barons were coming. . .

CHAPTER TEN

"Quickly," Jack said. "Form a circle, back to back. Keep your torches held out."

Shoulder-to-shoulder with Ben, Jack, Brother Lubek and Edwin, Emily braced herself to face this new enemy. Slowly, the black shadows thickened and pooled on the floor like spilled ink. The temperature in the chamber plummeted. It was freezing.

"Stay close to each other," Edwin warned.

The shadows shimmered and rippled, forming themselves into shapes which Emily could see were almost human. A head ... two arms ... broad shoulders, and then the shapes of seven men reared up in black shadow-form. The figures began to solidify, black against the red clay walls.

"They're taking human-form!" Emily cried.

"All the better," Ben said grimly. "That way we can fight them with fire – and win!"

"Grenades ready, everyone," Edwin muttered.

Emily gripped her grenade jar tightly in one hand and held her flaming torch high with the other.

Abruptly the black shadows rippled once more and seven men appeared.

Emily gaped at the arch-lampirs in surprise. They were younger than she had expected, and all of them were surprisingly handsome. Count Casimir Lampirska – she assumed he was the count, since he stood a little in front of his six barons – was the most dashing of all. He had piercing blue eyes, a thin nose and long, dark hair which swept back from his forehead as if he'd only just brushed it. Like his barons, the count was lavishly dressed in a long, dark red tunic, belted at the hips with a length of polished silver chainmail, encrusted with sparkling black gemstones. His feet were encased in chainmail boots with sharp spurs, and a black velvet cloak was fastened loosely around his shoulders. Emily could see a diamond pendant on a gold chain glittering in the hollow of his throat.

Count Casimir flexed his shoulders and stretched a little, like a man awakening from a long sleep. With an amused expression, he stared at the group behind the flaming torches. And the group stared back, half-mesmerized.

These are definitely not the sort of lampirs we're used to dealing with, Emily thought. And then she did the only thing she could think of: she hurled the torch in her hand straight at Count Casimir. The flames swept an orange arc through the air, sparks flying.

With the amused expression still on his handsome face, the count reached up and caught the torch in one hand. His fingers closed around the burning tip. For a moment, flames flickered between his fingers, and then they were extinguished.

The count's smile widened. He brushed his hands together carelessly as if the flames had been no more than a vague annoyance. And Emily realized that the arch-lampir was immune to fire.

"Uh-oh," muttered Jack. "Now what?"

"We get out of here," Ben said urgently.

"We need daylight," Emily put in breathlessly, as they launched themselves towards the archway to the second chamber. "Natural light will force them into shadow-form, and we'll be safe."

Together, they dashed through the vaulted chambers, the flickering light from their torches casting dancing shadows on the black marble, on the caskets, and on the gleaming white bones. Almost tumbling over each other in their haste, the group hurtled up the stairs and finally burst out into the main body of the church. Halfway down the nave, daylight slanted in through the grimy stained-glass window.

"Keep going!" Edwin cried, urging them on.

Emily ran, glad of her breeches so that she could move freely. She could hear Jack and Ben right on her heels. The doorway with its half-rotten wooden doors was an uneven rectangle of cold, white light in the near-distance. She saw the crumbling tombstones in the graveyard beyond.

Then, abruptly, a shadow passed across the doorway and the remnants of the rotten doors exploded in a cloud of dust. A gigantic figure stood there, framed against the daylight. Over two metres tall with a cadaverous white face and eyes of hollow, burning steel, Roman Cinska glared down the aisle at the group of friends running towards him.

Appalled, Emily skidded to a halt and Jack careered into her from behind. He grabbed her arm to steady her, and then stepped protectively in front of her with a look of utter horror etched across his face.

"It's Roman!" Ben said hoarsely.

"Back!" yelled Edwin.

As one, the group wheeled around, with Emily desperately looking for another way out. The stained-glass window, perhaps. . . ?

But Count Casimir Lampirska and his six barons were now ranged across the aisle behind them, blocking the route to the window. Their silver chainmail and fabulous gemstones glittered in the torchlight.

A shaft of dusty daylight slanted down from the window, lighting up the sparkling diamond pendant that nestled in the hollow of the count's throat. Emily felt her stomach lurch as she realized that the arch-lampirs were in human-form, despite standing in full daylight!

"It cannot be. . ." breathed Brother Lubek.

"I reckon the rules of the game have just changed," Jack said flatly.

Emily glanced over her shoulder at Roman Cinska. He still stood in the doorway, impossibly tall, his steely eyes burning bright with triumph.

The friends were trapped between two titanic forces of evil – and there was no escape.

CHAPTER ELEVEN

Ben watched in horrified fascination as Roman Cinska spread his arms wide, threw back his head and laughed. The sound echoed eerily around the inside of the church. A pane in the stained-glass window abruptly shattered.

"I am the Saviour of the Seven!" Roman said with a roar. "I have released you from your eternal sleep, my brothers." Arms still flung wide, he drew himself up, gazing down the aisle of the church at Count Casimir and the barons. "I am your new overlord," Roman continued. "Kneel and rejoice!"

"Oh dear," Brother Lubek whispered fearfully as he translated for the friends. "I fear they are going to join forces. Oh dear me. . ."

And then came a rumbling sound, like distant thunder. Ben looked at Count Casimir and saw that he was *laughing*. The arch-lampir's black hair rippled over his shoulders as he threw back his handsome head and bellowed with mocking laughter. Sharp-looking fangs glittered between his unnaturally red lips.

Suddenly the sound was shut off, and the count straightened up, his face icy. He turned to stare straight at Roman Cinska, and crimson fire seemed to flash in the depths of his blue eyes.

Then Count Casimir Lampirska raised one hand and lightly – so lightly that Ben wasn't even sure he'd heard a sound – snapped his fingers.

Gazing at the doors of the church, the arch-lampir locked stares with Doctor Roman Cinska. "The Seven do not *kneel*, old man!" the count said, in a voice that simmered with suppressed rage.

And at that, Ben felt the earth beneath his feet begin to shake. From outside the church came the sound of galloping hooves and the high-pitched whinny of horses. Ben exchanged a puzzled glance with Jack and Emily.

All three of them turned to stare towards the doorway.

Beyond Roman Cinska's towering frame, seven huge and powerful horses thundered towards the church. Ben saw at a glance that these were not like any horses he had ever seen before. Black as ebony, their outlines seemed to shift and shimmer like smoke. Ben realized that they were made of shadow, like lampirs caught in daylight! The horses' eyes burned red like fire, in hollows of coal-black shadow, while their hooves were bright balls of crimson flame.

The seven shadow-horses came hurtling towards the doors of the church. As they drew closer, Count Casimir gave another snap of his fingers. Immediately, the shadow-horses plunged into physical form, solid and black as night. They came galloping through the doorway in a column, pulverizing Roman Cinska beneath their iron-clad hooves.

Ben made a grab for Emily, and all five of the friends leaped away from the aisle and out of the path of the oncoming horses.

The huge beasts thundered past, the buckles on their elaborate black leather saddles rattling, empty brass stirrups jumping. Their powerful muscles rippled beneath their gleaming, jet-black coats as the horses snorted and pranced, rearing up to paw the air in front of the count and his barons.

The count reached up and seized the bridle of the largest horse. With a single fluid movement he leaped up into the saddle. The horse reared again, its nostrils flaring. The count laughed triumphantly, keeping his seat with practised ease. Then the beast's front hooves came down so heavily that a stone slab on the floor beneath it cracked from side to side.

The six barons were also in the saddle now. They wheeled their mounts and spurred away down the aisle, galloping out of the church without a backward glance.

"The daylight simply doesn't affect them," Edwin remarked incredulously.

"Must be all them weird experiments and rituals they did," Jack muttered.

"Black magic. . ." whispered Brother Lubek.

"Let's go and see where they're going!" Ben cried, and he dashed down the aisle towards the door with Emily at his heels.

Outside, a chill wind bit through Ben's clothes as he hurried across the graveyard, following the track that the horses' hooves had churned in the half-frozen earth. The hoofprints disappeared at the graveyard gate, and Ben wondered whether the Seven had switched to shadow-form for speed.

Shading his eyes with one hand, Ben looked to see which direction the arch-lampirs had taken. A narrow, rocky track curved towards the south and west, away from the village and up into the mountains. Black shadows flickered along it, moving unnaturally fast: the Seven! In the blink of an eye they had rounded a rocky bend and vanished.

Where are they going? Ben wondered. But as he gazed upwards, past the track's winding course, he knew.

Castle Lampirska was perched high on its crag, a black silhouette against the pale winter sky. Earlier, the ruined castle had been dark and obviously abandoned. But now it looked different, Ben thought. Flickering golden light danced in the windows, as if a thousand candles had been lit all at once.

Bats still wheeled and circled the crumbling towers, but the castle had come to life.

* * *

101

Beside him, Emily was staring up at the castle too. Then she turned to Ben. "We'd better go back and see what's happened to Roman!" she said with a sigh.

They hurried back across the graveyard and entered the church to find Brother Lubek, Edwin and Jack bending over Roman's broken body.

"He's seems to be shrivelling away. . ." Jack remarked.

Even as he spoke, Roman's head lolled to one side. The skin of his white face seemed to shrivel and shrink until it was so tight against his bones that Emily thought it would split. Then dozens of tiny dark cracks began to appear all over his body. They quickly spread, widening until his bones showed through. His dead eyes gazed blindly from the sockets, then they too shrivelled, turned liquid and seeped away.

"What's happening to him?" whispered Ben.

"He's disintegrating," Emily said. "Like the other lampirs do when they've been burned."

Roman Cinska's teeth turned yellow and dropped from his jaw. His hair withered and went grey, falling out in handfuls. And finally, the friends watched in horrified fascination as his body collapsed in on itself, leaving nothing but a pile of silvery ash.

Without warning, a chill wind whipped in through the open doorway of the church and the ash began to lift, swirling into the air in a million tiny fragments. Soon there was nothing left of Doctor Roman Cinska but a dark smudge on the stone floor.

"Guess he weren't the Saviour of the Seven after all," Jack said bluntly, straightening up and brushing some of the ash from the front of his coat.

"I'm glad his soul can now rest in peace," Emily replied, moving towards the doorway. She gazed up at the mountains, where the ruins of Castle Lampirska loomed. The golden lights had been extinguished now, and the castle looked dark and empty once more.

"We'd better head back to the village," Jack said, coming to stand beside her. "We should warn Pavel and the others that their troubles ain't over."

CHAPTER TWELVE

That afternoon, the ditches around the village were filled
to the brim with a mixture of oil and tar. Wagons were
loaded with torches, the end of each one wrapped with
tar-soaked cloth to make it burn faster and longer.

Jack was standing beside one of the wagons with Ben,
Emily and Edwin. Nearby, Pavel, Brother Lubek, and
some of the other villagers were busy strapping rope
around the handles of the torches to make firm
hand-grips.

"Seems to me there's something we ain't thought of,"
Jack said suddenly.

"What's that?" Emily inquired.

"Count Casimir Lampirska is immune to flame," Jack
pointed out. "We all saw him grab that torch you threw
at 'im. And it didn't burn 'im! So we're here, scurrying
around, making torches and filling the ditch with oil. But
what if 'e just walks through the fire, calm as you
please?"

"You're right, Jack," Edwin said. "But we still have to keep the ordinary lampirs at bay. And they *do* burn!"

Brother Lubek translated for the nearby group of villagers, who exchanged concerned glances. After a moment, Pavel spoke quietly in Polish to the young monk.

"Pavel is saying that none of the legends has ever mentioned immunity to fire," Lubek explained. "He is suggesting that it was just a lucky grab for the count, that maybe Lampirska was wearing gloves that stopped the flames from burning him?"

Jack shook his head. "No," he said firmly. "Tell Pavel not to kid himself. The count weren't wearin' gloves."

"He could have a point, though, Jack," Edwin said reasonably. "Perhaps it *was* a lucky grab."

"Maybe," Jack said. But he wasn't convinced. "It wouldn't hurt to have a back-up plan."

"What *kind* of plan?" Ben asked thoughtfully. "We don't know anything about the count, so we don't really know what we're dealing with."

"If only we'd brought the Dhampir Tome with us!" Brother Lubek said with a sigh.

"We don't need the Dhampir Tome," Emily said. "We have all the information we need, right here."

Jack shot her a questioning glance and she smiled at him. "The village elders," she said simply. "Old Roza, and these men working on the torches with Pavel. They're a walking, talking Dhampir Tome!"

"You're right, Em," Ben said, brightening. "We need to ask them to tell us everything they can remember about the way dhampirs fought, and how they trapped the count."

Later, in Pavel's house, over a meal served at sundown by Yelena and Daria, they did just that. The friends learned that the arch-lampirs could change from human-form to shadow at will, unlike their ordinary lampir servants who were forced to take shadow-form during the hours of daylight. And when they were in shadow-form, the count and his barons could move unnaturally fast, easily able to outrun men and horses.

"I remember my great-grandmother told me this," said one wizened, white-haired old man, who Jack thought looked about a hundred years old. Brother Lubek translated his words. "She said that the Seven could move more quickly than the human eye could follow!"

"But what are they afraid of?" Ben wanted to know. "Can you remember anything? Even something small might give us a clue as to how we can fight them."

There was a lot of muttering and conferring over this question, and Roza frowned deeply.

"There was the hair," the old woman said at last. "You remember, Yelena?" She glanced up at Pavel's wife as Brother Lubek translated. "We always used to cut the hair from the heads of lampir plague victims, after they had died."

Yelena nodded, looking slightly shamefaced. "We would plait it and make it into bracelets," she explained. "It was said that this would protect us. But when we lost two young people in a single raid – both of whom were wearing hair-bracelets – we knew it was only an old wives' tale."

"A myth!" Roza said, rocking gently back and forth on the rocking chair. "Like so many of the old stories." She tutted and shook her head. "There was talk of jewellery, once. My father told me when I was a girl. 'Roza,' he said to me, 'promise me that you will wear your mother's locket every day. Never take it off!' Of course I wear it still." Roza fished a small, tarnished silver locket from the collar of her high-necked black dress. "Much good it does me. Wearing a piece of jewellery that belonged to someone who succumbed to the plague for protection – such nonsense!" She chuckled.

"Oh, but it's not!" Emily exclaimed. "The jewellery really does work. We've seen it!" She turned to Jack. "Tell Roza about your ring, Jack."

So Jack explained about the gold ring he wore on his middle finger. It had been his friend's grandmother's wedding ring, but the old lady had died of lampir plague. She was one of the first victims in London. The ring had protected Jack from lampir attack many times during their adventures, most recently at the Monastery of St Wenceslaus when even Roman Cinska – half-lampir, half-human – had backed away from the sight of the gold band gleaming on Jack's finger.

"It really works?" Roza asked in astonishment. Her eyes twinkled with delight as she clasped her silver locket tightly. "Praise be!"

"There's your back-up plan, Jack," Edwin Sherwood said with a smile. "Jewellery. Every person in the village needs to find and wear a piece of jewellery that once belonged to a victim of lampir plague!"

"You forget how poor these people are," Brother Lubek said hesitantly. "I doubt there will be enough jewellery for everyone. . ."

"That's true enough, but we must do something," Pavel muttered. "I will send someone to spread the word that if anyone has such a piece of jewellery, then they should wear it!"

He spoke to a few of the younger village men, who nodded and slipped quietly out into the cold. Just as the last man closed the front door behind him, Jack saw the orange blaze of the setting sun as it dipped behind the rooftops.

"It's getting dark," Pavel said. He glanced at Edwin. "Will you take first watch with me tonight?"

Edwin nodded. "Of course," he said. "I'll take a handful of men and stand guard over the western-most ditch."

"We'll help," said Emily standing up.

Ben and Jack nodded in agreement, and before long the friends were taking turns to patrol the outskirts of the village.

But no lampirs came that night. And the ruined castle in the mountains, high above Ornak, remained mysteriously dark.

It was the same for the next three nights.

"Why don't they attack?" Jack asked on the fourth day after Roman's death. It was mid-afternoon, and he and Emily were standing in the square by the stone cross. They'd been checking and rechecking the wooden torches that were ready for use at a moment's notice. But, so far, none had been necessary, and the ditch had not been lit.

"It is not so strange," Pavel said as he came to join them. "Often lampirs do not come for several nights running."

Jack glanced across the square to where Ben was sitting on the doorstep of one of the timber houses. Little Florian was crouched at his side, watching with enormous dark eyes as Ben demonstrated how to fit an arrow on to a homemade bow. The arrow was blunted by a wad of cotton fabric wrapped around the tip.

"You fit the arrow like this," Ben was saying. "And you get someone to light the tip for you, so that it's flaming. And then you shoot – like this."

Ben loosed the arrow, and Jack watched it fly across the square. It hit a sack of turnips which Ben had propped up as a target outside Pavel's house.

"We got him!" Ben exclaimed, punching the air.

Florian leaped to his feet and punched the air too,

whooping with delight. "We got heem!" he yelled, mimicking Ben.

"Good shot," Emily called to her brother, grinning widely. "If that arrow had been lit, we'd be having roast turnips for tea!"

Yelena, Pavel's wife, appeared in the doorway of her house and beckoned them all inside. She had made a huge jug of hot apple cider. Jack took a sip and found it was delicious, sweetened with honey and spiced with cinnamon. It seemed to warm him right through, and he knew he'd be glad of that when night fell and the temperature dropped below freezing, as it had done each night that the friends had been in Ornak.

Just then, Edwin and Brother Lubek came indoors with Pavel, all of them unwinding the scarves from their necks. Brother Lubek crossed to the fireplace and held his hands out to the warmth.

"The pedlar has just stopped in the square," Edwin told them all. "He's come to deliver fresh supplies of oil for the ditches, and a hundred metres of tarred cloth so that we can make more torches."

"That's all very well," Emily said, shrugging off her coat. "But we haven't even used the ones we've already got." She frowned as she hung her coat on the back of her chair. "This waiting is horrible."

"When the fighting starts, we will wish we could go back to the waiting," Pavel said with a grunt.

"That's if there *is* any fighting," Ben put in. "There's

been no sign of life from the castle for days. I'm beginning to think that Lampirska and his barons have gone."

"No," Emily said, shaking her head. "He's not going to leave the territory he's hunted for centuries."

Ben shrugged. "He might, if he's afraid of the villagers. After all, they defeated him once, with the help of the dhampirs. Perhaps he's gone somewhere to find victims who are less likely to defeat him again."

Jack sipped his hot apple cider and listened to the conversation as more villagers came in through Pavel's front door. They stamped snow off their boots and blew on their hands to warm them. Yelena and Daria weaved back and forth through the crowd. Their colourful embroidered skirts swung around their ankles as they poured drinks and handed out *bialys*, little flat Polish bread rolls, filled with fried onions and poppy seeds.

Outside, the sun slipped below the rooftops and darkness began to close in. The men of the village began to arm themselves, tucking knives into their belts and testing the rope grips on some of the wooden torches. Their faces were grim as they gathered in groups, murmuring in low voices. Some of them wore pieces of jewellery – talismans taken long ago from relatives who had died of lampir plague.

Pavel began to give orders for the watch. "Once again, Edwin will take four men to the western ditch," he said. "I will take four men to the eastern, while Galus and Gerik patrol the borders."

Galus and Gerik, Jack saw, were two brawny men with protruding foreheads and flat, squashed-looking noses. Their powerful shoulders threatened to burst the seams of their thick sheepskin jackets. They looked like a pair of bulls, and so alike that Jack guessed they must be brothers.

"What about us?" Ben asked, brushing *bialy* crumbs from his fingers.

"For you, there is sleep tonight," Pavel said.

And when the three friends began to protest, the head villager held up his hand for silence. "I want you to rest properly, and be ready to take first watch tomorrow evening. These sleepless nights are beginning to take their toll on all of us, and we can't run the risk of anyone falling asleep at the vital moment! We must begin to take turns – one night on watch, one night off."

"All right," Jack said, and he had to admit even to himself that he felt tired. Sleeping fitfully during daylight hours was beginning to take its toll, just as Pavel had said.

When the men had gone, trooping out into the gathering twilight, Jack glanced at Emily, Ben and Brother Lubek. "I wish we had more than fire and jewellery to fight with," he muttered.

"Yes," said Ben with a grimace. "If only we had a dhampir to lead us into battle!"

"But the dhampirs are all gone," Emily murmured.

Jack turned to Roza. "You said that there was once a

dhampir family in Ornak," he said, waiting for a moment as Brother Lubek translated his words into Polish. "Is there really none of their line left?"

Roza gently rocked her chair back and forth. "There was one," she said, gazing into the fire with a faraway look in her eyes. "But he turned away from that path long ago."

A coal in the fireplace popped. Jack glanced at the window and saw a full moon had risen in a sky of the deepest blue. Pavel's wife Yelena sat down at the table beside him and reached for a *bialy*. She broke the bread roll in half and began to crumble it nervously between her fingers, talking in Polish to old Roza.

Eventually Roza nodded. "Yelena says, remember when you first arrived and asked us if anyone had ever left Ornak?"

Jack, Ben and Emily nodded when Brother Lubek had translated her words. And little Florian, sitting at Ben's feet, nodded too, mimicking Ben's every move.

"Pavel mentioned a man called Stefan. . ." Jack said slowly, trying to remember the details.

"That's right. Poor Stefan Kowalski had already lost two children in lampir raids," Roza said. "So he and his pregnant wife Celestina turned away from Ornak. And in doing so, they turned away from their dhampir heritage – because Stefan Kowalski was the last of the dhampirs. But he swore that his dhampir blood was cursed, because he was not able to save his own children!"

"Maybe we could find him?" Ben said eagerly. "Ask him to come back?"

But Roza shook her head. "Sadly that is not possible, my boy," she said. "Stefan and Celestina were drowned in the cold Baltic Sea. Their ship sank, two days out of the port of Danzig." Roza sighed and shook her head mournfully. "Nobody knows whether the baby was born before Celestina was killed, but even if it was, it seems likely that the poor child would have perished with its parents."

The old woman stared into the flickering flames of the fire for a moment. Then she sighed and glanced up at the friends with a hopeless expression in her eyes. "But one thing is clear," she said sadly. "These days, there are no dhampirs left to save Ornak!"

CHAPTER THIRTEEN

Ben woke suddenly in the darkest hour of the night. He was cold. No matter how many layers of clothes he wore to bed, the Polish winter still managed to chill him to the bone.

But it wasn't just the cold that had woken him. Ben suddenly became aware that he could smell smoke. A glance at the window showed an orange glow in the sky. The ditches were on fire! He could hear panicked cries, and the confused shouting of the men of the watch.

He leaped out of bed and threw some more clothes on. Lampirs had attacked – and he'd been sleeping!

Suddenly there was a frantic knocking on his bedroom door. Ben threw it wide and saw Daria standing there, her face white with shock.

"They come," she said, using the simple English she had picked up over the past few days. She held out a knife. It was long and sharp, encased in a leather scabbard, and he guessed it had once been her husband's hunting knife. Her husband, Ben knew, was dead, killed in a lampir attack when Florian was a baby.

"Thank you, Daria," Ben said. With the knife in his hand, he ran from the house. In moments he was out in the square, where a pall of thick smoke stung his eyes.

"Over here, Ben!" came Jack's frantic yell.

Jack had been sleeping too. Ben could see that his friend was still wearing his pyjama top, the blue-striped sleeves at odds with the thick sheepskin waistcoat Jack had shrugged on in his haste to get outside.

Something sliced through the air, and Ben reached up to catch the unlit wooden torch that Jack had thrown to him. He touched the tar-stained end to a brazier that glowed in the middle of the square, and then ran full-tilt towards the eastern-most ditch. Pavel was there, struggling with a lampir that had obviously taken him by surprise. Beyond him were five more snarling lampirs.

The western ditch was already burning, Ben saw, the flames running quickly round the village. But they wouldn't reach the eastern stretches quickly enough! He could feel a rumbling in the earth beneath his feet, and suddenly, out of the darkness, burst the huge and terrifying black shadow-horses. They switched into solid-form as they bore down on the village, red eyes rolling and nostrils breathing flames. Count Lampirska was in the lead, his black hair rippling as he spurred his horse on towards the ditch.

"Oh, no, you don't," Ben hissed. He dived forwards and touched his flaming torch to the oil in the ditch. It ignited immediately. Ben felt the heat scorch his face as the flames roared upwards in a wall of fire. The inferno spread and quickly joined the fire coming round from the west.

Abruptly, the village of Ornak was surrounded by a wall of flame. And the count and his barons were still on the other side.

"Well done, Ben!" Emily yelled. Wearing breeches and a green woollen jacket, she was standing with a bow in her hands. A flaming arrow was poised on the string, and abruptly she loosed it.

The arrow flew through the night air, whistling as it dipped and found its target – the lampir that was fighting with Pavel. Just as the creature opened its mouth to tear the head villager's flesh open, the arrow buried itself in the lampir's back.

Instantly the creature turned into a blazing pillar of flame, and Pavel leaped away to safety.

"Nice work!" Jack said, shooting Emily an admiring glance.

But Ben was staring past Emily in horror. His little friend, Florian, had followed him, and Ben could see him running down the main street, his bare feet flashing on the cold ground.

"No, Florian!" Ben yelled, shaking his head and gesturing frantically. "Go back into the house!"

But Florian didn't understand. He kept running towards Ben, a dogged expression on his face. And just at that moment, a terrible laugh echoed through the night behind Ben.

Ben wheeled round and stared, appalled, as Count Lampirska's horse flew over the ditch, straight through the wall of flame, and landed with a heavy thud in the village.

The arch-lampirs had come to Ornak.

Panicking villagers scattered, screaming, as the count and his barons thundered across the town square.

But the villagers couldn't move fast enough, and Ben saw the barons pluck two of them from the ground. One was a woman, who screamed as a powerful hand grabbed her by her long hair. The other was a young man, barefoot and still in his nightshirt.

The arch-lampirs separated, slipping into shadow-form again as they spurred their mounts through Ornak's narrow streets.

The count, however, remained in the square. He sat astride his black horse, his lips drawn back from his pearly-white fangs as he smiled at Ben, Jack and Emily. The sounds of fighting carried from the other side of the village, and Ben could hear panicked voices rising in shouts of alarm.

Emily fitted another flaming arrow to her bow and quickly loosed it at the count. But he simply swatted it away as if it was a fly. His horse pranced sideways, its long tail swishing.

Then the count turned his mount towards Ben.

"*Nie!*" A tiny figure launched itself across the square, and Ben realized it was Florian. The lad positioned himself in front of Ben, his arms spread wide as if to protect the older boy. "*Nie!*" he shouted again. *No!*

The count laughed coldly and gazed down at Florian with amusement. Then he bent low in his saddle and scooped the little lad up with one arm.

Ben dragged his knife from its scabbard and darted towards Count Lampirska, as Jack began to run across the square to help. Florian cried out in alarm as the arch-lampir wheeled his horse around.

"Florian!" Ben yelled desperately. He lunged forwards and sliced his knife across the count's arm.

But the count seemed unconcerned, and the next moment, he was gone. His horse had leaped straight through the wall of flame, and Ben could only watch in helpless rage as the arch-lampir thundered away from the village.

Behind him rode the six barons, each with a victim flung across their saddle. The terrified screams of the captives echoed on the night air.

CHAPTER FOURTEEN

"Where's Edwin?" asked Emily, a short time later. She was standing in the doorway of Pavel's house.

The moment the count and his barons had gone, Pavel had called a council of war. Dawn was just breaking in the east, so five men of the watch were left patrolling the burning ditches, while everyone else made their way across the square to Pavel's house.

Emily scanned the room again. She saw a host of familiar faces: Brother Lubek, old Roza, Florian's mother, Daria – who was deathly-white, but remarkably calm considering her little son had just been kidnapped. But there was no sign of Edwin.

"Where's Uncle Edwin?" Emily said again.

There was a moment of silence. Emily thought several people were avoiding her gaze.

Jack and Ben came into the house behind her. "Yes, where *is* Edwin?" Jack asked with a frown.

This time Pavel stood up. "He was taken," the head

villager said hoarsely, his Polish accent stronger than ever. His shoulders were hunched and his face looked grey in the cold light of dawn. "He fought bravely, but he was no match for the Seven."

"*Taken?*" Emily echoed in horror. She exchanged a stricken look with Jack and Ben.

"Don't worry, Em," Ben said, clenching his fists. "We're going to get him back!"

"Too right, we are," Jack muttered.

Emily nodded and began to speak, but raised voices on the other side of the room drowned out her reply.

"I think we should all leave this place!" bellowed one of the villagers, a small man with slightly bulging eyes who Emily knew was called Boris.

Brother Lubek quickly translated.

"Ornak is a place of death," Boris was grumbling loudly. "We have no chance here now that the count has been released!"

"I am with Boris," agreed another man. "I have lost a child tonight – my only son. I do not want to see any more of my family snatched by those blood-suckers."

"Leaving Ornak will not help," Daria said suddenly. She pointed through the window to where the ruined castle was perched high on its rocky crag. "Our enemy is up there. We should go after him and fight, not run away!"

"Daria's right," Emily said, gripping her bow tightly. "We must climb the mountain."

"Climb the mountain?" Boris sneered. He spat into the fireplace. "You will be climbing to your death!"

"That's a chance we'll have to take," Emily said firmly. "I'm not going to run away while Edwin's a prisoner up there. Now who will come with me?"

"Well, we will, obviously," Jack said, and Ben nodded firmly.

"I'm with you, of course," Brother Lubek added with a nod.

"And I shall come too," Daria declared. "I have already lost a husband. I will not give up my son as well!"

"I will come," Pavel put in gruffly. He glared around the room at the other villagers. "Who else?"

But everyone shuffled their feet nervously, and refused to meet Pavel's gaze.

"No one?" Pavel barked. "You leave all the dangerous work to women, young people and monks, eh?" With a derisive snort, he marched across the room and yanked open the drawer of a wooden dresser. "Here is gold for anyone who volunteers," he said curtly, fishing out a pouch which bulged with coins.

A few of the villagers muttered amongst themselves, and finally two men raised their hands. Emily recognized them immediately as Galus and Gerik, the two burly brothers in sheepskin waistcoats and baggy woollen trousers.

"Anyone else?" Pavel asked. He stared around at his

people, his dark eyes flashing angrily. "Then Galus and Gerik will share the contents of this pouch when we return. And the rest of you," he added in a low voice, "are cowards."

"Not cowards," Boris said with a grunt. "Wise men." He jerked his square chin at Pavel derisively. "What are the chances of you and your little army coming back, eh? You will be eaten alive."

"I hope it won't come to that," Pavel said quietly.

Ben glanced at Emily and Jack. "We should leave immediately," he said. "It's going to be a long hike up to the castle."

"Just what I was thinking," Emily agreed grimly. "We need to make the most of the daylight."

"I'll go and fetch the horses," Brother Lubek offered.

Roza stood up, her knees creaking. "I may be too old to fight," she said. "But I can help to gather weapons for you."

"And food," added Yelena. "I will wrap some *bialys*, and also fill goatskins with water for you to drink."

Despite Boris's loud grumbling, many of the other villagers also proved willing to help the travellers prepare. When Emily emerged into the square ten minutes later, with a knapsack on her back and her bow in her hand, she found a crowd of well-wishers gathered around the horses.

"Take no notice of that Boris," one of the men called, handing Jack an old sword and Ben an axe. "You won't be eaten alive if you arm yourselves."

"Here," said another. "Take my knife. I use it for cutting wheat in the harvest season, and the blade is sharp enough to slice off the count's head if he so much as looks at you!"

"And here is my bill-hook. . ."

Everyone was speaking so fast that Brother Lubek was barely able to keep up with the translations.

"I have brought three hammers. . ."

"And take these wooden torches. I have tied them in bundles of five so that you can strap them to your saddles."

Laden with weapons and muffled to their eyes in fur and sheepskin, the eight travellers left the village just as the morning sun was beginning to climb in the pale winter sky.

As she led her horse over the barren ground past the old church where Roman Cinska had met his death, Emily found herself casting uneasy glances up at Castle Lampirska. The ruin was a constant brooding presence that seemed to watch the travellers as they made their way upwards.

"The castle don't seem to get no closer," Jack said, after an hour's steady climbing. He glanced back down to where the village was nestled in the frost-bitten lowland hills. The landscape looked like part of a grey-and-white map which had been unrolled far beneath them. He could see the river where they had tried to outrun the lampirs a few days ago, and beyond it the thick green forest of Sosnowy Las.

The village looked tiny, and Jack found that if he held out his hand with his thumb extended, he could cover all of Ornak's little houses. All that was left visible was the blackened ditch, like a halo around his thumbnail.

"It's much colder up here," Ben said, hitching his canvas knapsack higher. His breath was a cloud of white in the chilled air.

"Yes, my eyelashes have frozen," Emily observed, rubbing her eyes with a gloved hand.

They were following a wide, steep track which twisted and turned its way up the mountain, past banks of crisp white snow and rocky outcrops strung with glittering icicles. Bare trees were dotted here and there, stretching black skeletal branches up towards the grey sky.

The track had obviously once been a road, perhaps the main carriageway to the castle. But, here and there, rockfalls had scattered stones across the track, and the horses had to pick their way over the uneven ground. A bitter wind whipped flurries of fallen snow up to sting the travellers' faces.

Jack plunged onwards up the track. The group had four horses which they had decided to lead rather than ride, because the saddles were heavily-laden with weapons, bundles of torches, and goatskins of water. Jack's horse, Apollo, had gone lame, and Jack had reluctantly left him in the care of one of the villagers, a gruff but friendly man called Michal.

"Look after him," Jack had said to Michal as he left the little barn where Apollo was stabled with Michal's two donkeys. And Michal had nodded and given Apollo an apple.

Now Jack was leading Edwin's horse, and he hoped its next rider would be Edwin himself.

Jack glanced up at their destination once more. The ruined castle was still some distance away, and behind it the mountains rose dark and brooding against the sky. Behind the peaks, thick grey cloud rolled in.

"Snow is threatening," Pavel said. "And darkness will come early tonight. We must hurry!"

No sooner had the head villager spoken, than snow began to fall, swirling on the freezing air. A shrill wind howled in the cracks and gullies. Heads bent, the travellers pushed on. An hour went by, maybe more. Jack, who was in the lead, felt he was losing track of time. His feet ached and the cold was beginning to numb his bones. A glance back at Emily showed him her nose was red and her eyes watered from the icy blasts. Ben's cheeks were turning blue, and Brother Lubek looked pale and haggard. Perhaps they would have to stop soon – or turn back and try again the next day.

But Jack thought of Edwin lying wounded somewhere, and little Florian at the mercy of the count and his barons, and gritted his teeth against the cold. There might not even *be* a next day for the captives!

Turning a corner, Jack saw that Castle Lampirska had

disappeared. It was hidden by a bleak, rocky outcrop. In front of him, part of the road had slipped down the mountainside, leaving a sheer precipice which fell away to jagged rocks below.

"Careful here," he called, turning back to warn the others.

Abruptly something black flew up out of the rubble beside him, making him jump. Leathery wings rustled alarmingly, as the creature wheeled away up the mountainside. Edwin's horse reared in shock, slipping on the perilous ice. Jack grasped the reins and hauled the beast away from the edge of the precipice just in time.

Ben stared after the flapping black shape. "A bat!" he cried in surprise. "What is a *bat* doing crawling about in broad daylight?"

"Strange, isn't it?" Emily muttered, her eyes narrow and alert. "They don't usually choose such exposed spots to roost in."

Jack shuddered. "Reminds me of an old enemy of ours," he muttered darkly. "Camazotz had his vampire servants slip into bat-form at the drop of a hat." Then he frowned and glanced up, his gaze following the route the bat had taken. "Hope it weren't spying on us. . ." he added thoughtfully.

The next twist in the track led them around a rockfall and out on to a bleak plateau. There at last, dead ahead, was Castle Lampirska. It was bigger than Ben had expected, a stark assortment of watchtowers, spires and turrets which stretched upwards into the overcast sky. All of it was surrounded by a thick wall which had been hewn from the sheer black rock of the mountainside.

"At last," said Ben, with a sigh of relief. He pushed back his sheepskin hat and rubbed his cold face with the back of his hand in an effort to get the blood flowing.

"Don't get too excited," Jack muttered. "We've got to get across *that* first!"

Ben looked to where his friend was pointing. When he saw what "*that*" was, his heart sank. The way to the castle's imposing gatehouse was barred by a deep ravine which fell away in a sheer drop.

"There's a drawbridge," said Brother Lubek helpfully.

But the drawbridge was a narrow, rickety-looking thing which didn't seem as though it would take the weight of one person, let alone eight and four horses.

Ben exchanged a keen look with Jack. "We'll have to try," he said. "There isn't any other way."

"If we go across one at a time, we might make it," Jack agreed with a nod.

"I'll go first," said Ben firmly. He took a step towards the drawbridge.

"Tie this rope round your waist," Emily said, handing him a coil of rope which had been looped over the pommel of her saddle. "We'll fasten the other end to a rock this side of the ravine. And if you do the same when you get to the other side, we can use it as a hand-rail."

"And if I fall," Ben said with a stiff grin, "at least you'll be able to haul me back up on to firm ground!" He handed the reins of his horse to Daria and knotted the rope firmly around his waist, then waited while Jack tied the other end to a stout rock and tested its strength by hauling back on it with all his might.

"All right," Jack said at last. "But be careful."

Ben's heart pounded as he stepped on to the drawbridge. The wood creaked and shifted and he caught his breath for a moment. Then he took another step, leaving firm ground behind him. One glance down showed him the yawning chasm beneath the splintered drawbridge. *Put one foot wrong. . .* Ben thought, and then firmly closed his mind to the possibilities.

The rotten wood groaned as he made his way gingerly across the bridge, but it held, and soon he was almost on the other side. Six more steps . . . five . . . four. . .

Suddenly a loud *crack* echoed across the mountainside, as a plank of wood gave way beneath Ben's foot. Ben threw himself forwards on to another section of the drawbridge as he felt himself start to fall. The little group on the cliff-edge gasped, as Ben scrambled to get his feet back up on to the remaining planks. He could see part of the broken wood spinning away into the ravine below him.

Carefully, he crawled the last few metres across the chasm and on to the solid ground of the far side.

Ben heaved a great sigh of relief.

"Be careful," he called back to the others, as he freed himself from the rope and tied it securely to a rock. "You'll need to go slowly, and test each step in case there are more rotten parts."

"I'll go next," he heard Jack say. "And I'll take one of the horses. . ."

Emily followed Jack, leading her horse on a short rein, and talking gently to calm the mare. Then came Daria, Pavel with Ben's horse, and Brother Lubek leading his.

As the brothers, Galus and Gerik, took turns to cross the drawbridge, Ben studied the front of the castle. The drawbridge led to a large archway through the castle wall. Beyond that was a courtyard, where there seemed to be dozens more archways leading off to other areas.

The front of the castle rose like a sheer cliff-face, interrupted here and there by arrow slits and tall arched windows which glittered with thick green glass. Above each window was a gargoyle with a scowling face and bulging eyes.

Stone steps carved out of the mountain rock led up to a huge front door, its sturdy oak surface studded with enormous rusty nails. As soon as the last person had crossed the drawbridge, Ben strode forwards and lifted the iron latch.

The door swung open silently.

Ben glanced at Jack, who was tethering the horses.

"Take these," Jack said, and tossed Ben a long, lethal-looking knife and a couple of torches. "I'm right behind you."

"So am I," Emily added, her bow in one hand and a torch in the other.

The others armed themselves and gathered behind the three friends: Brother Lubek, pale but composed; grim-faced Pavel, his black moustache crusted with frost; Daria, muffled in sheepskin and scarves; and, finally, the two burly brothers, Galus and Gerik, carrying armfuls of weapons and torches.

Taking a deep breath, Ben nodded at them all. Then he stepped inside Castle Lampirska.

CHAPTER FIFTEEN

Ben stepped over the threshold into an enormous hall which was dusted with snow and strung with glittering icicles. His footsteps echoed eerily, and he had the sense he was stepping into a great, icy tomb. A feeling of uneasiness swept over him.

"It's so quiet in here. . ." came Emily's voice from behind him, as she and Jack stepped inside. She had lit her wooden torch and the flames threw light up on to the walls, where rich tapestries glowed with forgotten grandeur. Faded crimson, jade-green and sapphire-blue seemed to ripple and dance as Emily moved closer.

Daria came in next, stamping her heavy boots to get the snow off them. She stood staring around the great hall with a look of awe on her face.

And no wonder, thought Ben. *This place is incredible!*

A vaulted ceiling soared above their heads, high as the inside of a cathedral. In the centre of the room was a huge, dusty table surrounded by elaborately carved chairs. Draped with a sumptuous gold-embroidered cloth, the long table was laden with silver platters, jewel-encrusted candelabra, and tall crystal goblets with fragile stems. Frozen cobwebs were strung like pearl necklaces from goblet to goblet.

"This hall is fit for kings," murmured Pavel. "Not just lords."

Behind him, Galus and Gerik merely grunted. Brother Lubek made his way cautiously through the doorway and entered the castle with a weapon in each hand.

All around the hall Ben could see marble archways leading to other parts of the castle. He picked one. "Shall we start through there?" he asked, pointing with the sharp tip of his knife.

Jack and Emily both nodded, and the friends carefully made their way through the arch and up the steep staircase that lay beyond. Brother Lubek and the others followed them, their torches chasing back the shadows. Every step of the way, Ben was aware of portraits hanging on the wall. Generations of stern-looking Lampirskas stared out of the paintings, brooding on their former glories.

The staircase led to a long gallery with doors leading out of it. There was a large arched window at the far end, its glass long since gone, and rays of daylight slanted down on to the flagstone floor, making the drifts of snow glitter beneath the windowsill.

"We'd better see what's in each of these rooms," Jack

said, lifting an iron latch quietly. The hinges of the heavy door creaked as he pushed it open.

The first room was a bedchamber, big enough to hold Ben's own bedroom six or seven times over. An enormous, mildewed tapestry covered one wall, and a thick green velvet rug hushed their footsteps as they advanced into the room. Set against another wall was a huge four-poster bed, curtained with ragged silk and fraying gold braid.

"Nothing in here," Brother Lubek said. "No signs of life at all."

They moved on to the next chamber, and then the next. Every room was the same – faded and spoiled, yet somehow still grand.

The last chamber was the grandest of them all. Almost as big as the great hall downstairs, it occupied one corner of the castle and extended out into a circular tower, where four or five high arched windows let the daylight stream in.

The friends made their way into the centre of the bedchamber, gazing around at the mirrors and glorious paintings which lined the walls. Some of them were speckled with age, while others looked almost new. A richly-draped four-poster bed stood against one wall, its sides curtained with thick folds of blood-red velvet.

Ben began to move across to the window, but a startled cry stopped him in his tracks. He glanced back over his shoulder.

Emily was standing by the four-poster bed. She had just drawn back the curtains and the fabric was so rotten it had come away in her hand. But that wasn't what had made her cry out. . . .

Count Casimir Lampirska reclined on the bed, his body making barely a dent in the black silk sheets.

Ben felt his mouth go dry.

The count's hands were folded across the front of his dark red tunic and his eyes were closed. His cheeks looked stark white and his unnaturally red lips were parted slightly, to show sharp, pearly fangs. Despite his handsome face, the count looked like the personification of evil, and Ben suppressed a shudder.

"Let's finish him now," Jack whispered, his hand tightening on the axe he was carrying.

But before anyone could move so much as a muscle, the count's piercing blue eyes snapped open. He sat bolt upright – making Emily gasp and step back in surprise – and surveyed them all for a moment,

"Uh-oh," muttered Jack. His voice held an edge of panic. "'Is Lampir-ness is awake!"

At the sound of Jack's voice, the count hissed. His gaze fell on Jack for a moment – then, before anyone could act, he rippled into shadow-form and abruptly vanished.

Emily gaped at the empty space where the count had been. He'd simply disappeared! She blinked and looked again, but his sinister black shadow was nowhere to be seen.

"What do we do now?" she said, clenching her fist.

"He'll be back," Ben replied grimly. "Probably with all his lampir barons in tow!"

"We don't have much time, then," Emily said decisively, her mind racing. "I think we should split up if we want to rescue the others and get out of here before nightfall!"

"I don't see that nightfall will make much difference," Jack muttered. "The count seems to be able to move around without worrying what time o' day it is!"

"But Lampirska is still a creature of the night," Brother Lubek pointed out. "Darkness makes him stronger – we saw that when he was able to ride into the village and snatch men, women and children. He came by night!"

"That's true," Pavel said with a frown. Emily saw him glance at the window. "I would say it is twelve of the clock, so we have perhaps four hours of daylight left. Emily is right – we must split up."

Ben nodded. "We'll take different sections of the castle to search, and then meet up in the courtyard in about three hours. We need to be away from here before sunset." He turned to his sister. "Emily, you'd better take Galus and Gerik with you." He glanced at the two brawny brothers. "You'll be safe with them to protect you."

"All right," said Emily. "And you go with Daria. The two of you can try to find Florian together."

"Then I shall accompany you, Ben," Brother Lubek said. "It will be easier if I can translate for you and Daria."

"That leaves me and Pavel," Jack put in. "And the ring." He frowned for a moment and then twisted Molly's gold ring off his finger. "Which I'm going to give to Emily."

"No!" Emily protested. "You need it, Jack."

"I want you to have it," Jack said firmly. "If you ain't going to be in sight, then at least I'll know you've got something other than the Brawn Brothers to protect you!"

"Take it, Em," Ben urged. "Otherwise neither Jack nor I will be able to concentrate properly on the search. We'll be too busy worrying about you!"

Emily rolled her eyes. "All right," she said impatiently. "But only to shut the both of you up." She jammed the gold ring on her index finger. "Now let's go!"

Ben's group made their way down a spiral stone staircase to the dungeons, deep underground. Ben was in the lead, and he held his torch out in front of him to light the way.

"Ssh!" said Ben, frowning. He was sure he had heard something – some movement in the darkness far below. "Did you hear that?"

The others listened. But there was nothing.

They continued on down the winding staircase, the darkness deepening all around them.

And there it was again, a shuffling sound. . .

"It could be the captives," Brother Lubek said hopefully. "The dungeons are the most likely place to keep prisoners, after all."

But the moment Ben turned the last corner of the twisting staircase, he knew that the shuffling sound had not been made by the captives. A dozen lampirs rippled out of the darkness below and took on human-form.

Brother Lubek let out a horrified shout. "It is daytime. Why are they in human-form?" he yelled.

"Because it's as dark as night down here," Ben said. "They can take whatever form they want!"

"There's too many to fight," Brother Lubek cried.

"Back!" Ben shouted. "Back up to the daylight!"

They scrambled back up the winding staircase, round and round to a small landing where a ray of daylight slanted in through a high arrow slit. The lampirs surged some way up the stairs after them, but stopped before they reached the daylight.

A guttural lampir groan echoed up the staircase, and Ben's skin went cold. "How many lampirs do you think are down there?" he whispered.

"Sounds like hundreds," Brother Lubek replied hoarsely.

"They must be guards," Ben muttered. "Which means

there must be something down there that's worth guarding!"

"Prisoners?" whispered Brother Lubek.

All three looked at each other grimly.

"We attack!" Daria said in her broken English.

Ben nodded. "But we have to get past this lot first," he said. "And the best way to do that is to set fire to them."

Propping his knife against the wall, Ben shrugged off his knapsack and quickly handed out three little grenade jars. "Throw them hard down the stairs to the very bottom, so they smash when they hit the floor," he instructed, and Brother Lubek quickly translated for Daria. "Then we toss a lit torch down the stairs, and stand back while everything goes up in flames!"

Daria nodded and touched her lips to her jar. "For Florian," she murmured.

"One . . . two . . . three. . . Now!" Ben cried.

With a clatter, the earthenware jars hit the stone floor of the dungeon and smashed into tiny fragments, spilling oil everywhere. Immediately, Ben tossed his torch down and then shielded his face with his arm as the oil ignited.

The stairwell filled with thick, choking smoke. Lampirs twisted and screeched as flames leaped up their bodies, racing over their ragged clothing and dry flesh. A few of them turned and ran back into the dungeons.

"After them!" yelled Ben, dragging his knife out of its scabbard.

He launched himself down the winding stairs,

stamping out flames and kicking at burning scraps. Whatever he touched disintegrated into ash, and he was able to plough on down into the dungeons. Brother Lubek was right behind him, a fresh grenade in his hand. Daria wielded her torch like a sword, swiping it from left to right as all three friends burst into the chamber at the bottom of the staircase.

The chamber was round, about ten paces in diameter, and its curving walls oozed moisture. A large metal grille was set in the middle of the stone-flagged floor – the entrance to the castle sewers, Ben guessed. Two long, dark corridors opened off the chamber, one on either side. They were lined with barred cells.

Feeling a rush of hope, Ben darted into one of the corridors and peered through the thick iron bars of the first cell. The place stank so much that he had to hold his breath. The floor was ankle-deep with green, slimy water. The walls dripped. But there were no prisoners.

"Ben!" Brother Lubek called, his voice loud in the semi-darkness.

"I'll check the other cells," Ben yelled back to the others, hurrying forwards.

"*Ben!*" Brother Lubek shouted again.

This time, something in the young monk's voice made Ben turn and look. And what he saw made his skin turn cold.

A horde of new lampirs was emerging from the

corridor on the other side of the chamber. Some of them were in human-form, snarling and gnashing their fangs. Others were hulking black shadows, rippling across the stone floor and walls to surround the three companions.

Ben, Lubek and Daria quickly moved back-to-back to form a tight unit. They held their flaming torches out in front of them and prepared to do battle.

But they were far outnumbered by the lampirs. Ben braced himself as the first one lunged towards him. . .

"Down here, Pavel," yelled Jack. "There's a door to the outside, and I can see some outbuildings!" He felt a wave of hope as he wrenched open the door which led from the castle kitchens to the outdoors.

Frozen air rushed in from outside.

"That is perfect place for locking up captives," Pavel said in his strongly-accented English. He peered past Jack's shoulder at the outbuildings. "You were right to come and look here, Jack!"

Weapons clutched tightly in their hands and torches flaming, the pair hurried outside into the cold daylight. The yard was about a hundred paces square, cut into the glittering black rock of the mountainside, and a large archway connected it to the main courtyard at the front of the castle.

There were three outbuildings. The first yielded nothing but shovels and piles of wood for the castle's enormous fireplaces. The next was obviously an old stable, divided into stalls. Mildewed hay was scattered on the floor here and there.

"Empty," Pavel said heavily, holding his torch up high so that light reached into every corner.

"And no sign that anyone's been in here recently," Jack agreed.

They moved on to the last outbuilding, and just one look at the big double doors made Jack's heart begin to pound with excitement, for the doors had been fastened with a long chain as thick as Jack's arm. He and Pavel exchanged a keen glance.

"There is something in there," Pavel muttered, unsheathing the sword that was hanging from his belt.

"Something," Jack agreed, hope surging through him as he handed Pavel his torch to hold. "Or some*one*!"

He swung his axe and brought it crashing down on the thick chain. Sparks flew as metal struck metal. Two more blows, and finally the links of the chain sprang apart.

Jack wrenched the chain from the door handles and pushed the doors open. The inside of the building was thick with shadows, but as his eyes adjusted it was plain to see that there were no captives. Just an ancient, once-grand carriage, with large, spoked wheels and peeling paintwork.

"Nothing," Jack said, feeling disappointed.

He made his way back out into the yard and frowned up at the walls of Castle Lampirska. For a moment he tried to imagine that he was the count. . . Where would he hide a group of prisoners?

Jack's roving glance fell on a semi-circular tower built into the sheer black rockface of the mountainside. It had no arrow-slits or windows, just a thick wooden door, banded with iron. There was no visible chain or lock, but other than that it looked like an ideal place to keep prisoners.

Jack shot an enquiring glance at Pavel, who nodded.

They approached quickly, weapons in hand. The door to the tower swung open easily, allowing them both to step into the single room beyond. Rusting weapons lined the stone walls, and benches stood in rows as if soldiers had once gathered here, waiting for orders from their feudal lord.

But now it was empty.

Or was it? As Jack held his torch out, he caught a movement out of the corner of his eye. His stomach lurched and he gripped his axe tightly, bracing himself as one ripple became two, and then ten. In the blink of an eye, a dozen shadows were swooping across the floor towards him.

"*Lampirs!*" Pavel hissed, holding his torch out in front of him with one hand, while his other hand tightened on his sword.

"Keep the door open," Jack said urgently. "Make sure the daylight keeps them in shadow-form!" He swung his torch wide, chasing the shadows back with the flame.

But Pavel must not have understood, Jack thought. Because from behind him came the hollow sound of a boot kicking against wood, and the door crashed shut!

Jack blinked as he was plunged into darkness. There wasn't an arrow-slit or a window to let in the smallest ray of natural light – which meant that the lampirs were now able to take human-form. A lampir snarled and rippled into physical form. Jack dashed his torch against its chest and the creature burst into flames.

"Pavel!" Jack yelled. "I said to keep the door open!"

But then he saw that the head villager was still there beside him in the middle of the chamber, his face stark with terror in the orange firelight.

Jack frowned. If it hadn't been Pavel who shut the door, then who else could it have been?

The temperature in the garrison-room dropped abruptly. Jack shivered in the cold and the hairs on the back of his neck lifted. Sensing a presence behind him, Jack turned.

A fair-haired man stepped out of the shadows behind the door, his chainmail boots scraping against the stone floor. He was tall and handsome, dressed in a beautiful sky-blue silk tunic and a short velvet cloak fastened with a sparkling jewelled clasp. Perfect, pearly fangs glistened as he smiled.

Jack realized he was face to face with one of the six barons.

CHAPTER SIXTEEN

Jack swung his axe at the baron. But the arch-lampir simply laughed and snatched the weapon from Jack's grasp. With amazing strength, he snapped the sturdy axe-handle in half and tossed it aside.

Yelling, Jack lashed out with his torch. But the baron took that too and extinguished it with a single breath.

Nice! Now I ain't got any weapons, Jack thought, feeling suddenly vulnerable. Instinctively he backed away.

Pavel rushed forwards, wielding his flaming torch like a battering ram. He ran straight at the baron, but without warning, three lampir foot-soldiers materialized in front of the arch-lampir, rippling up from the thick shadows on the ground. Snarling, they reached for Pavel, but the head villager was too quick. He stabbed his torch quickly, setting fire to one lampir after the other, until three columns of twisting orange flame lit the room.

More lampirs solidified into human-form and Jack braced himself for their attack. But they unexpectedly veered away from him and went for Pavel instead. The head villager swung his sword, slicing it through desiccated flesh and brittle bone.

Jack turned to grab one of the rusty weapons hanging on the wall beside him. The closest was a sword. He snatched it down, praying that the blade was sharp, and slashed at the nearest lampir.

The creature had once been a rich man, judging by the opulent velvet coat which hung in shreds from his hulking shoulders. But now he was withered and half-rotten, with earth from his grave clogging his beard and eye-sockets. He snarled as he moved towards Jack, but then, abruptly, the lampir cowered and drew back, one arm flung up as if to protect himself.

It's almost as if he's scared of me, Jack thought. *Even though I ain't wearing the ring to protect me.*

Across the other side of the garrison, Pavel did battle with his torch, desperately setting fire to lampirs as the baron watched with a look of mild amusement on his face. Meanwhile, Jack lunged towards another lampir.

Immediately the creature cowered away from him.

"Come on!" Jack yelled. "What are you scared of?"

"They are scared of *you*," Pavel cried, his voice puzzled.

But there wasn't a moment for Jack to think about what that might mean, because suddenly a blade sliced through the air, centimetres from his ear. The baron had seized his own weapon of choice from the wall. It was a scimitar, a wide curved blade which glittered like burnished gold as it caught the torchlight.

Jack ducked away from the razor-sharp blade. But the baron leaped forward and kicked at Jack, his shiny chainmail boot just catching the underside of Jack's chin. Jack's head snapped back, and pain flooded his jaw as he staggered and fell.

On the other side of the garrison, Pavel was yelling as he set fire to lampirs left, right and centre.

Jack found himself on hands and knees, without his sword. He'd dropped it, and, with a laugh, the baron now kicked it out of reach.

Pain seemed to fill Jack's brain and he shook his head to clear it. He tasted something bitter and metallic, and knew that his mouth was full of blood. Had he lost a tooth?

Before Jack could put a hand to his mouth and check, the baron was standing over him, his scimitar raised. All he had to do was sweep it downwards, and Jack would be dead.

Jack's street instincts took over and he ducked away fast. "Don't expect me to make this easy for you!" he said. He snatched at the baron's booted foot and jerked it hard. The baron gave a yell as he lost his balance and fell on his back. Jack scrambled to his feet and stood over the arch-lampir, blood dripping from his mouth. He stamped hard on the baron's hand to make him loosen his grip on the scimitar.

And suddenly the tables were turned! Jack had the hilt of the broad, curved scimitar clutched tightly in his fist. He held the weapon high, prepared to bring it slashing down. "Any last words, Baron?" he asked grimly.

Across the room, Pavel stabbed his torch at the last of the lampirs, turning the creature into a towering pillar of raging flame.

Jack leaned over the baron and stared down into his enemy's face. Blood was pouring from his mouth now, and he could feel the jagged edge of a tooth. He knew it ought to hurt, but the pain would come later when this was all over.

Crimson blood dripped on to the baron's silk-clad arm. The baron screamed in horror and Jack felt a small surge of satisfaction.

"Ruined your fancy tunic, have I?" he asked mockingly.

But it was more than that. . .

Even as Jack watched, the sky-blue silk seemed to disappear. The baron screamed in agony as the blood began to sizzle against his skin. A terrible smell filled the air – burnt fabric and seared flesh – and the arch-lampir's arm slowly but surely dissolved. Jack gaped. Soon all that was left was bone, white and gleaming. And then that was gone too, and the baron was clutching the stump of his elbow.

The arch-lampir stared up at Jack in terror. *"Dhampir!"* he hissed.

And abruptly the baron's entire body dissolved. His flesh sizzled and fell away, until there was nothing left but a pile of silvery ash.

Jack wiped the blood away from his mouth. He noticed that all the lampirs had been defeated. The floor was littered with the ash of a dozen or more burnt creatures.

"Did he say 'Dhampir'?" Pavel asked, staring at Jack in wonder.

Jack blinked. "Er, I d-don't know. . ." he stuttered. *Had the baron really said "Dhampir"?* he wondered. Certainly his blood had destroyed the baron, and Jack knew from reading the Dhampir Tome that the blood of a dhampir was poisonous to a lampir. . .

Abruptly, everything began to click into place in Jack's mind. He now understood why the lampirs had been afraid of him earlier, even though he no longer wore Molly's ring.

But if he was a dhampir, then it was no wonder lampirs had always been terrified of him. Jack's heart began to pound as he realized that perhaps his old friend, Filip Cinska – and, more recently, Roza from the village – had been right. *Perhaps I really do have Polish blood in my veins!* Jack thought.

He swallowed hard, his mouth suddenly dry. Along with Ben and Emily, he had always assumed that it was

Molly's ring that kept the lampirs away. If a person wore a piece of jewellery that had once belonged to a victim of lampir plague, then the jewellery protected the wearer. That was the rule; it had said so in the Dhampir Tome.

But what if that was just another old wives' tale? Another myth? The Dhampir Tome was a frustrating mixture of accurate information, legends and folktales. The friends had always known that.

Suddenly, Jack felt a rush of panic, because if it hadn't been the *ring* protecting him, then Emily was in danger – especially if she relied on the ring for protection at any time!

Jack stared at Pavel, his mind racing. "We have to find Emily," he said. "Fast!"

Emily's footsteps were hushed by acres of plush red carpet. She had found her way to an enormous room where bookcases lined the walls from floor to ceiling. On the spines of a thousand books, gold-tooled lettering gleamed under the bright orange glow of Galus and Gerik's flaming torches. Velvet armchairs were grouped around an enormous fireplace. Between two tall, arched windows stood a small table bearing a crystal decanter and four crystal goblets.

But, Emily realized with a pang of disappointment, there were no prisoners. She glanced out of one of the windows, and saw that the pale winter sun had broken through the clouds. It was beginning its descent towards the horizon now, and she knew that time was beginning to run out.

I hope the others are having more luck than I am, she thought.

Just then, she saw something flicker out of the corner of her eye and she turned quickly towards it. A dark figure was materializing out of a shadow on the carpet at the far side of the room. He solidified into a man, even as he strode towards her.

He was wearing a black velvet tunic over chainmail boots with spurs and pointed toes. The sheen of his long black hair caught the light as he moved, and his perfect fangs glittered in a triumphant smile.

With a jolt, Emily recognized Count Casimir Lampirska.

"Przybyl demon!" yelled Galus, his voice harsh with panic. And Emily knew just enough Polish to realize that he had said: *The demon is here!*

She was scrambling to fit an arrow to her bow when the count reached Galus and Gerik. He shot out a perfectly-manicured hand, ruby rings flashing, and gripped Galus by the throat.

With his piercing blue eyes still holding Emily's gaze, Lampirska simply clenched his fist and crushed Galus's neck, killing him instantly.

"Nie!" screeched Gerik. For a moment the brawny villager gaped down at his brother's lifeless body, crumpled on the carpet. Then, with a yell, Gerik dropped his torch and fled from the room in terror.

In that moment, Emily knew she must face the count alone.

Her mouth went dry with fear. She tossed her useless bow aside and scrabbled for the knife that was tucked in the belt of her breeches. But she couldn't free it; the hilt was caught on something.

Instead, she held up her hands, and her last hope for survival glinted on her finger: Molly's ring.

The count looked at the gold band, glittering on Emily's hand. But his stride did not falter as he advanced across the room towards her.

CHAPTER SEVENTEEN

Instinctively, Emily backed away. But there was nowhere to go. She felt herself back up against a bookcase. Her spine pressed against a dozen leather-bound books. Still, she held her hand out in front of her, hoping to ward off the count with Molly's ring.

But the count did not seem to care.

Emily's heart began to race. She twisted the ring from her finger and held it up like a shield. But the count just kept on coming.

Finally, she tried to duck away, but the count was upon her, his fingers closing around her wrist. Emily shuddered at his touch. The arch-lampir's skin was ice-cold, like death itself. Panicking, Emily tried to free her hand. But his grip was like a steel vice.

Count Casimir's mouth curved in a smile as he slowly brought Emily's wrist up to his mouth.

Without warning, the count bit into Emily's sleeve, shredding the dark-green fabric and tearing back her cuff to expose the skin beneath. Emily struggled wildly, but it was no use. The count had her pinned against the bookcase. He smiled and examined her wrist for a moment, apparently fascinated by the thin blue veins just visible beneath the skin. Then, with the speed of a snake, he struck.

The needle-sharp points of his perfect teeth sliced through Emily's skin, and her red blood began to flow. Then, Count Casimir reached for one of the crystal goblets on the nearby table. He pressed the lip of the glass to Emily's wrist, and carefully collected her crimson blood.

When the goblet was half full, the count held it up to the light, tilting it slightly. The blood gleamed like liquid rubies, dark and mysterious. With a smile, the count passed the goblet beneath his nose and inhaled, like a wine expert savouring the bouquet. Finally he raised the goblet to Emily in a silent toast . . . and drank.

Emily shuddered and tried to tear her eyes away from his, but the arch-lampir seemed to have the power to hold her gaze. She found she *couldn't* look away!

An expression of intense curiosity crossed Count Casimir's handsome face as he drained the glass. Emily saw that a droplet of blood remained, poised, on his lower lip, and she gazed at it in horrified fascination.

The count carelessly threw away the goblet, which shattered on the floor, and licked the blood from his lips. "Delicious. . ." he said crisply, startling Emily with his perfect English. "The best I have tasted for quite some time!"

Emily held her breath, staring up at him. *Will he let me go now?* she wondered. *Or will he bend forwards and sink his perfect fangs into my throat? Well, I won't go without a fight!*

She flashed the count a defiant glare, and he laughed. The sound echoed around the room, growing louder and louder until Emily wanted to scream and cover her ears.

Then, abruptly, Lampirska stopped laughing. He reached out and grasped Emily's chin, tilting her head back so that he could stare down into her eyes. His face was so close that she could feel his frozen breath on her face.

"Welcome to my castle, Miss Emily Cole of London," he said slowly. His voice was low and dark and dripping with evil. "What an interesting life you have led. You are certainly more spirited than my usual prey."

He frowned suddenly, his eyes turning dark as new-forged steel. "I see you are no stranger to death," he hissed. "You have done battle with blood-hunters before – and won!"

Emily realized that, somehow, drinking her blood had given the count a strange knowledge of her past. It was almost as if he could read her mind, and see her memories. The image of Camazotz – demon-god and vampire – seemed to hang in the air between them for a moment. Then Emily blinked and the image was gone.

Count Casimir's hand tightened on her wrist and she gasped with pain, dropping Molly's ring.

"Now, Miss Cole," the count said thoughtfully. "What am I going to do with you?"

Ben swung his torch at the lampirs and glanced across at Brother Lubek.

The monk held his torch out in front of him with a trembling hand, but his face was full of determination and Ben knew at a glance that he was prepared to fight to the death.

"We not give up!" Daria shouted angrily in her halting English. "We not die!"

"We aren't going to die," Ben told them both firmly. "There must be some way out of this." He could feel an indentation in the stone floor beneath his foot and knew it was the metal grille set into the floor of the underground chamber. *Let it be loose,* he prayed silently. *Loose, and not too heavy for me to lift!*

"Keep them busy," Ben said urgently to Lubek. "I need to lift this grille."

Brother Lubek glanced down and took in the significance of the metal grille. "A trap!" he murmured, a look of excitement crossing his face. "Good idea, Ben!"

Immediately, the young monk jabbed the blazing tip of his torch at the nearest lampir, setting fire to the creature's long white hair. A terrible shrieking sound echoed around the dungeons as the lampir burned, popping and crackling like fireworks.

Taking her lead from Brother Lubek, Daria darted forward and burned two lampirs in quick succession, deftly stabbing her torch left and right.

Behind them, Ben hauled at the grille. It was heavier than he had expected, and the effort made his arms burn as he dragged it aside. But at last the wide black hole beneath the grating was revealed. Ben leaped backwards.

"Let them come!" he urged the others.

Lubek and Daria checked behind them, then sprang nimbly back over the hole. The lampirs hurled themselves forwards in pursuit – and abruptly fell straight down into the castle sewer. They began to struggle slowly to their feet, momentarily dazed by the fall. But those behind didn't falter, or reach down to help their comrades. They just advanced blindly, their milky-white eyeballs fixed on their prey. Groaning and snarling, clawing the air with their sharp black fingernails, they surged forwards and stumbled into the yawning hole, one after the other.

Soon all of them were in the sewer.

"Help me get the grille back across," Ben said, heaving at the heavy iron grating with all his might.

Brother Lubek and Daria lent their strength, and within moments the grille was in place and the lampirs were temporarily trapped.

"Grenades!" Ben urged. "And then torches. Quickly, before they switch into shadow-form and escape!"

Immediately, Lubek and Daria dashed the last few earthenware jars down on to the iron bars. They broke, and flammable oil splashed down on to the lampirs beneath. One touch of a flaming torch was all it took to ignite the lot of them, and within moments the dungeons were filled with thick, bitter-smelling black smoke.

Screams filled the air, but Ben and his companions turned their backs on the enemy and went to search the prison cells.

The captives were in the last cell of the corridor from which the lampirs had emerged. The door to the cell was open, but the seven slumped figures within were chained to the walls with thick iron shackles around their wrists and ankles. They were cold and shivering. Several of them moaned as if in pain.

Daria gave a cry and rushed to the smallest figure. "Florian!" she cried, and scooped the little boy into her arms. Her fingers fumbled with the iron pins which fastened his shackles.

"Mama?" Florian croaked in disbelief. He smiled weakly as he recognized Ben's face in the torchlight. "Ben!"

Seeing the boy's cracked lips, Ben untied the goatskin bottle of water from his belt and handed it to Daria. "Brother Lubek, tell her to make sure he just takes sips at first," he said. "Big gulps might be too much for his stomach."

Hurriedly, Ben moved on to free the rest of the prisoners. There were three other children besides Florian, all of them weak and barely conscious. Brother Lubek knelt over one of them. She was a young girl with long fair hair. Her cheeks were pale and hollow, and her lips had turned blue.

"Is she all right?" Ben asked anxiously.

"She will be," Brother Lubek said firmly. "But we need to get her out of this place as soon as we can."

The three adults who had been kidnapped from the village were right at the back of the cell. One of the men was badly injured – dried blood was crusted across the front of his torn shirt. He managed to lift his head as Ben approached, and Ben felt a mixture of relief and horror when he saw that it was Edwin.

"Uncle Edwin," he said breathlessly, dropping to his knees and struggling to unfasten the shackles which held his godfather. "Are you badly hurt? Do you think you can walk?"

"I believe so," Edwin said, his voice cracking. He managed a grin through parched lips. "I am glad to see you, my boy!"

Edwin was soon free and Ben moved on to the next of the adult prisoners – a young man called Szymon who was weak but only slightly injured. The third prisoner, however, had not fared so well. Brother Lubek was kneeling beside her with a sombre expression on his face.

"I'm afraid she's dead," he said softly to Ben. "Drained of blood. Look!"

The young monk pointed to the young woman's neck, and Ben saw a ragged wound across her throat from which lampirs had drunk all her blood.

"There's nothing we can do for her now," Ben said sadly. "I suggest we get the other prisoners up into the daylight, and then find Jack and Em. We should have just enough time to make it back to the village before sunset!"

"Where do you think she can be?" Pavel said, as Jack's search for Emily grew increasingly desperate.

They had searched every room, from the kitchens to the bedchamber where they had first stumbled upon Count Casimir Lampirska earlier that afternoon, and yet there was no sign of Emily.

Shadows thickened and shimmered around every corner. The wind sighed against the windowpanes. Jack could feel apprehension clawing at his stomach, but he tried to keep it under control. Emily was here somewhere, he told himself. It was just a case of finding her.

Eventually, after searching endless stone corridors and climbing up and down myriad flights of stairs, Jack realized he was now in the east wing of the castle for the first time. The doors to several rooms were open, and as he glanced in through the nearest door, his heart sank – a wooden torch lay on the floor!

Heart beating frantically, Jack motioned silently to Pavel. He pointed, to show he was going into the room, and then pressed his finger to his lips.

Pavel nodded to show he'd understood.

Then Jack held his sword out in front of him and stepped carefully into the room. He glanced quickly left and right, in case a lampir was lying in wait for him behind the door – he wasn't going to get caught the same way twice!

But the room was empty.

Relaxing just a little, Jack took stock. He was in a library, the walls lined with leather-bound books. The room was icy-cold. Rich silk curtains billowed across a partly-open window, and Jack noticed that the sun was beginning to dip towards the horizon.

In an hour or so it would be sunset, and Jack remembered that he and Pavel were supposed to be meeting their friends in the courtyard now. Perhaps Emily was safe and sound. Perhaps she would be there, in the courtyard with the others, waiting.

He was just about to leave the library when his glance caught something on the floor, glittering in a cold shaft of afternoon sunlight. Puzzled, he walked over to look.

"Broken glass," said Pavel, coming to stand beside Jack. "One of these perhaps?" he suggested, indicating the remaining crystal goblets on the small table.

"Yes. . ." Jack said slowly, because he'd noticed something red smeared across some of the shards of crystal. Something that looked remarkably like wine.

But no, Jack thought as he picked up one of the larger pieces and sniffed at the red liquid. *This ain't wine. This is* blood*!*

Frowning, Jack crouched down and picked up a shred of fabric that lay on the carpet amidst the pieces of glass. He turned it over in his hand, noticing the ragged edges.

"This has been torn from someone's sleeve. . ." he began to say to Pavel. But the words almost choked him, because all at once he recognized the woollen fabric as coming from the jacket that Emily had been wearing.

Jack straightened up and stared at Pavel in horror. "Something's happened to Emily," he whispered. "There's blood on the glass and this fabric is from her sleeve!"

"Blood?" Pavel muttered, looking concerned. "This looks bad, Jack."

Jack crushed the fabric in his fist and swore softly. "It's all my fault," he moaned. "She relied on the ring to save her – and the ring was useless!" He shook his head. "She should have run away."

Pavel suddenly stiffened, staring at something just out of Jack's field of vision. "Galus. . ." he whispered in horror.

Jack looked in the direction of Pavel's gaze and saw that the burly villager was lying half-concealed behind a big leather armchair. He could tell by the awkward angle of Galus's head that the man had been killed by a superhuman force.

Had Emily met the same fate? Just the thought of it made Jack burn with fury.

Across the room, the arctic breeze fanned the silk curtains and made them billow away from the window. Jack glanced up and saw a dark figure step from behind the curtain. Tall and lean, dressed in jewelled black velvet, Count Casimir Lampirska was unmistakeable.

And there was *Emily*, Jack realized with a jolt. The Count had one arm clamped tightly around her neck, and the other braced like a vice around her waist. He was holding her right off the floor, but she was kicking and struggling, her eyes wide as she stared desperately across the room at Jack.

Emily is alive! Jack thought in delight. But there was no time to dwell on that now. He had to help her.

Jack lunged across the room, sword at the ready. But the count was prepared. His body rippled and shimmered. Jack reached for him with a cry . . . but it was too late. The count had switched into shadow-form and disappeared.

And he'd taken Emily with him!

CHAPTER EIGHTEEN

Ben was in the courtyard with Brother Lubek and the freed captives.

Daria had Florian in her arms and several other children clung to her long, embroidered skirts. Edwin and the young man called Szymon were leaning against the courtyard wall, supporting one another. Both of them looked dazed.

Suddenly two figures burst out of the castle. Everyone looked up in alarm, fearing lampirs, but they relaxed when they saw that it was Jack and Pavel.

Ben was the only one who still felt anxious – a single glance at Jack's face had told him that something dreadful had happened.

He listened in disbelief as Jack quickly recounted the events in the library.

"He took her, Ben," Jack finished angrily. "The count changed into shadow-form and *he took Emily with him!*"

"We have to get her back," Ben said immediately.

"I'll help," Edwin put in, pushing himself away from the wall.

"But you are too weak," Brother Lubek pointed out, looking worried. "You are injured, Edwin."

"Besides, there is no time for rescue now," Pavel said gruffly. He glanced up at the sky. "Sunset is approaching. We have to get these people out of here while we still can!"

"I'm not leaving without Emily!" Ben said flatly.

"Nor me," agreed Jack.

"Nor me," Edwin added weakly. But, suddenly, the archaeologist closed his eyes and slid down the wall into a sitting position. Horrified, Ben and Jack rushed forwards and crouched beside him.

"He's unconscious," Ben murmured. He stared at Edwin for a moment, his mind reeling. Then he stood up and turned to the others. "It's a long journey down the mountainside," he said quietly. "You'd better start without me. I'll catch up once I've found Emily." And he began to stride across the courtyard towards the entrance to the castle.

Pavel blocked his way, looking exasperated. "Ben, you risk your own life by staying here!" he exclaimed.

"I'm not leaving without my sister," Ben replied stubbornly. "You go on without me."

"I don't think any of us can go anywhere," Brother Lubek said hesitantly. "There are eleven people here and only four horses. Some of the injured are too weak to walk. . ."

"Is hard to walk down mountain," Daria put in.

"But wait," Pavel said. "There is a carriage we can use!" He turned to Jack. "Remember, Jack? We found it earlier. It is very old, but the wheels are still good. If we harness our horses to the front, then we can carry everyone safely back to the village."

"A carriage?" Brother Lubek asked, his face brightening. "That is a stroke of luck. Show us where it is."

Ben nodded. "It's a good idea," he said. "Perhaps Pavel and Jack can organize the carriage." He put his hand on the hilt of his knife.

"Will you help us?" Brother Lubek asked.

Ben shook his head. "You don't need me," he said. "But Emily *does*." As he turned away, however, he found Jack gripping his arm tightly.

"Let's help Pavel and Brother Lubek to get the others on the road," Jack said quietly. "Then we can go and find Emily together!"

Ben hesitated, worried that he was wasting precious time. He wanted to find Emily immediately. But a glance at Pavel, Brother Lubek and Daria, struggling with the wounded prisoners, made him hesitate.

"C'mon," urged Jack. And Ben finally agreed.

Ben, Jack and Daria led the four horses through a

stone archway to the outbuilding where the carriage was housed, and began to secure them to the front of the carriage. Brother Lubek and Pavel carried Edwin between them and settled him on one of the bench seats inside the musty old coach, while Daria, Szymon and the children huddled round him.

Brother Lubek and Pavel climbed up to the driver's seat at the front.

"Come on, Ben," Jack said, swinging up beside them. "Let's get them on the road, eh?"

"But what about Emily?" Ben asked, confused. "You said we'd find her together!"

Jack leaned down and held out his hand to help Ben up. "And so we will, mate," he said with a grin. "Trust me."

Ben grasped Jack's hand and swung up on to the driver's seat. The carriage rolled forward with a jolt, and soon they were under the stone archway and back in the main courtyard once more.

"What about the drawbridge?" Ben asked, suddenly remembering that it stood between themselves and escape.

"You will see!" Brother Lubek said gaily. "Szymon and I – we fixed it earlier!"

"You fixed it?" Ben said with a gulp. "How?"

The young monk grinned but didn't say anything. He just watched Ben's face as the carriage rattled towards the drawbridge.

"You used the table from the great hall!" Ben exclaimed, impressed.

"Thank goodness for that," Jack said with a shout of laughter. "I wouldn't have fancied our chances otherwise!"

But even so, Ben noticed that everyone held their breath as the carriage clattered over the makeshift drawbridge.

The bridge held. And all at once the carriage gathered speed as the horses raced across the wide expanse of flat rock beyond and thundered on to the roadway. Ben clung on tightly, glancing back over his shoulder at the castle.

They were some distance from the Lampirska stronghold when Ben suddenly saw something that made his blood freeze.

Five barons in shadow-form, mounted on five shadow-horses, came careering out of the castle. The horses' fiery eyes caught the rays of the late-afternoon sun, and their black shadow-hooves blazed red with flame as they sped across the drawbridge in pursuit of the carriage.

"Faster!" yelled Jack, who had seen them too. He snapped the reins, whipping up the horses so that the carriage shot forwards.

Ben clung on to his seat as the carriage swung round a sharp right-hand bend. The wheels slid on a patch of ice, and for a moment, he had a horrifying vision of the carriage hurtling off the roadway and over the side of the mountain, plunging them all to their deaths on the jagged rocks below.

But Jack was in control. His feet were braced against the wooden boards and he was half-standing as he urged the horses on. On the other side of him, Pavel was muttering something in Polish, while Brother Lubek said a prayer.

"Here, let me help you," Ben said, reaching over to help Jack hold the reins.

Together they struggled to control the horses. The animals were clearly terrified, snorting and neighing, nostrils flared and manes flying. They were obviously aware of their unnatural pursuers.

Another glance over his shoulder showed Ben that the barons were still some distance away. But they and their mounts were still in shadow-form, rippling fast over the frozen earth as they veered round the twists and turns of the roadway. Behind them, the sun was now beginning to set, a fiery orange ball dropping towards the horizon.

"The next time we round a bend," Jack muttered to Ben, through gritted teeth, "we jump clear. You got that, mate?"

Ben nodded.

"We'll hide behind a rock, or a bush or something . . . and then as soon as the barons have ridden past, we'll go back up that mountain to find Emily."

"Got it!" Ben said firmly.

For a few moments, Jack's eyes were fixed on the road

ahead. Then abruptly he thrust the reins into Pavel's hands. "Drive," he said simply.

"*What?*" Pavel cried, staring at the friends. "What are you doing?"

"You can outrun the barons," Jack reassured him. "The coach is far enough ahead o' them. Now, drive!"

Pavel still stared at Jack in confusion, but Brother Lubek simply reached across and took control of the careering carriage as it neared the next bend. "You go," he told the boys. "Pavel and I will manage." The young monk fixed the head villager with a stern expression. "*Won't we*, Pavel?"

"Er, yes," Pavel responded. He glanced across at Jack and Ben. "Good luck."

The sun dipped behind the mountain and a single star glittered in the evening sky, as the carriage rattled around the bend.

"Now!" Jack cried.

Ben launched himself off the side of the wooden seat. For a moment he was aware only of a weightless feeling, of flying through space, of the wind on his cheeks. Then his breath was knocked from his body as he landed in a huge snowdrift. Powdery snow went up his nose and in his eyes. His hands were buried. He felt Jack land nimbly beside him, and then they were both scrambling behind a clump of scrubby bushes to hide.

A minute later, the five barons on their fiery shadow-horses came thundering around the bend like an evil, black avalanche. They brought the night with them, a thick blanket of darkness which blotted out everything.

Then Ben and Jack were alone.

CHAPTER NINETEEN

"The coast is clear," Jack muttered after a few moments.

Warily, the friends ventured back out on to the roadway. For a moment they listened for any sign that the shadow-horses were returning. But not a sound broke the stillness of the night. Up above, the ruined castle loomed over them, black against the deep blue of the night sky.

For a moment Jack thought that more stars had come out, but then he saw with a sickening lurch of his stomach that the castle had come alive – strange golden lights flickered in every window, and the strains of unearthly music began to carry down the mountain on a chill breeze.

He felt Ben nudge him. "Come on," said his friend. "Let's go and get Em."

Emily's quick glance moved from Count Casimir to the door and back again.

She was standing in the middle of a candlelit bedchamber, somewhere high in one of the round towers of the castle. A small fire crackled in the hearth, chasing away the cold.

All the elegant gilded furniture in the room had been fashioned to fit the curves of the rounded tower walls: the long, strawberry-pink velvet sofa, the dressing table, the full-length mirror edged with gold, and last of all, the enormous four-poster bed draped with dark blue silk curtains which were so long that they rippled on the floor in shadowy folds. *Everything is rounded, curved, feminine*, Emily thought. *This was a woman's room once. . .*

She looked at the window and then at the door. Both were firmly closed.

"There is no escape," the count said with a cold laugh, as he followed Emily's glances. "Do you think I would forget to lock the door? I, Casimir Ziemovit Lampirska, Lord of Ornak?" He shook his head, still laughing. "Oh, no, no, no! I cannot risk my guest of honour disappearing. For what use then would all my careful preparations serve?"

"Preparations?" Emily asked, intrigued despite herself.

The count swept low in an elaborate bow. "There is to be a banquet this evening," he told her. "A great feast!"

"And I'm the guest of honour?" Emily queried, swallowing hard. "I'd rather be excused, if it's all the same to you."

An expression of anger crossed the count's handsome face, but he swiftly masked it with another cold smile. "There are to be no excuses tonight, Emily Cole. You have no choice. You are my guest whether you like it or not."

He strode across the room and flung open the doors of an enormous, highly-polished wardrobe. Immediately, silk gowns and satin petticoats burst free, spilling across the floor in shimmering pools of crimson, daffodil-yellow and sky-blue. The count ignored them all, trampling the lovely fabric with his chainmail boots as he searched through armfuls of taffeta and gold lace.

At last he seized a white silk gown from the back of the wardrobe. It was beautiful, a long, low-necked gown with tight sleeves ending in long pointed cuffs which Emily knew would almost cover her hands entirely.

For a moment the count paused, burying his face in the soft, slippery folds of the dress. Emily heard him inhale deeply, as if he wanted to savour the scent that clung to the silken threads. Around the room, the candles plunged and guttered.

Then, abruptly, the count tossed the gown across the bed where it lay like a drift of snow. "You will wear this tonight," he said.

"I will not!" Emily argued defiantly. "I'm leaving, right now." She marched towards the door with her head held high.

But a pool of rippling black raced across the carpet ahead of her and the count materialized from his own shadow, barring the way to the door, his arms folded across his chest and a smile of cold amusement playing about his red lips.

"I do not give you permission to leave," he said quietly.

"I don't need your permission," Emily countered.

She dodged sideways, trying to pass him. But he was there in front of her, still smiling coldly. She tried again, the other way this time. Again he blocked her path.

Emily gave up and stepped backwards away from him, her hands held out placatingly. "All right," she said, deliberately making her voice soft and submissive. "You win. I'll put on the gown, but you'll have to give me a little privacy."

"That's better," Count Casimir said approvingly. "I am glad you have seen the error of your ways." He slipped a large, black, wrought-iron key out of the folds of his tunic, and held it up. "But don't forget that the door will be locked," he murmured. "So any attempt to escape will be fruitless." And, with that, the count rippled into shadow-form and slipped away beneath the door.

Immediately Emily ran to the door and lifted the latch. It was locked, just as he'd said. She cursed lightly and went to the high, arched window at the far end of the room. It opened outwards, and Emily put her head out and looked down the sheer side of the castle tower. It was dark now, and icy-cold. Bright silvery moonlight glanced off the jagged rocks far below.

No escape that way, Emily thought grimly.

Or was there?

Her gaze fell on a small balcony jutting out of the wall about three metres down. A tall, narrow window gave on to it, and it had been propped open slightly. A cold wind whistled through the elaborately-twisted wrought-iron railings.

Emily's mind raced. There was another room in the tower, directly below hers! If she could get down there, perhaps she could climb in through the window and then escape. Surely not every door in the tower would be locked?

Filled with steely determination, Emily looked around the bedchamber. *Sheets*, she thought immediately. *I'll tie them together and climb down.*

Feverishly, she stripped the big four-poster bed of its feather quilts. Then it was the work of moments to knot the ends of two sheets together. She fastened one end tightly to a bedpost and tossed the other end out of the window. Then she looked out to see how far her makeshift rope reached.

The tip just brushed the wrought-iron railing of the balcony.

"Perfect!" she said to herself.

Emily dragged a chair across to the window, hauled herself up and swung one leg over the sill. "Thank heavens for breeches," she muttered, and grinned at the thought of being able to tell Ben that she'd been right all along about the impractical nature of petticoats.

She glanced down before swinging her other leg over, and almost fell off the windowsill in shock!

Count Casimir was standing on the balcony directly below her, one hand on his hip and the other lightly holding the end of her sheet-rope.

"Going somewhere, Miss Cole?" he asked coldly.

He looked as if he'd been waiting there for her to make her move, almost as if he'd known what was in her mind. Again, Emily was struck by the fact that, ever since drinking her blood, the count seemed to have a sinister knowledge of her innermost thoughts.

Count Casimir was still smiling as he rippled into shadow-form and moved swiftly up the wall. With a cry of horror, Emily leaped off the windowsill backwards into the room. She landed awkwardly, lost her balance and sat down heavily on the carpet. Instantly she felt a chill in the air, and looked up to see the count now looming over her in human-form.

His sharp teeth gleamed as he smiled and held out his hand to her. "Allow me," he said smoothly.

Emily hesitated, staring at the open palm of his hand. There were no lines on it, she noticed. The skin was smooth and white. A dead man's hand. She shuddered and glanced up at his face again, finding her gaze drawn immediately to his piercing blue eyes.

"A lady," the count said softly, only just loud enough for her to hear, "will always allow a gentleman to come to her aid."

I might be a lady, thought Emily mutinously, *but you're certainly no gentleman.*

Nevertheless, she found herself placing her hand in his, almost as if she had no will of her own. His fingers closed tightly around hers and he drew Emily to her feet. She found herself face to face with the count. He stared into her eyes.

The room around her seemed to fall away as Emily became lost in the mesmerizing depths of Count Casimir's gaze. His eyes were fiery gateways to another world, heaven perhaps. . .

But no, Emily quickly reminded herself. *Not heaven. Hell!* She tried to look away, but found that she couldn't.

"If you are going to insist on being so terribly difficult, Miss Cole," said the count, "then I am going to have to hold you in thrall to me." He tipped his head to one side as if he was listening to something.

"Hush," he said softly. "Do you hear that?"

Emily could hear nothing but the crackle and spit of burning logs in the fireplace.

"That sound is the beat of your heart," the count continued.

Emily could feel his concentration focused on the pulse that fluttered in her neck, and suddenly found that she could hear her own heartbeat.

"There it is. *Ba-doom. Ba-doom. Ba-doom.* It is driving your fresh young blood around your body," Lampirska told her. He sighed and closed his eyes ecstatically. "Blood is life," he said at last.

And then he lowered his voice, slipping easily into his native Polish, and whispered words which seemed to slip like shadows through Emily's mind. He was so close that she could feel his freezing breath on her cheek, and his black hair brushing against her chin, like cold silk. Her head began to swim and her body felt so light that she thought she would float away. . .

Emily struggled, briefly. A small voice in her head told her that she should be strong, that she must not listen to the count's words. But his voice was a lullaby, soothing her frantic thoughts, and she no longer wanted to resist the hypnotic spell that Count Casimir Lampirska was slowly but surely weaving about her heart.

CHAPTER TWENTY

As Ben and Jack set off for the castle, Jack reached out and grabbed his friend's sleeve. "Ben," he said. "There's something I have to tell you before we go back up there."

"Go ahead," Ben said with a nod.

"I don't rightly know how to put it," Jack said awkwardly. As they walked along he kicked at a loose pebble with the toe of his boot. "You see, it's my fault that the count's got Emily—"

"No, it's not," Ben interrupted.

"Yes it is," Jack insisted. "I gave her Molly's ring to protect her."

"Then Em must have taken it off for some reason." Ben shrugged. "That's hardly your fault, Jack."

"You don't understand!" Jack looked suddenly exasperated. "The ring didn't work, because the story about a piece of jewellery protecting a person is just that – a *story*!"

Ben glanced sideways at his friend in confusion.

"What do you mean, Jack?" he said at last. "The ring has always worked for you."

"But it wasn't the ring, Ben. It was *me*. You see, I had to fight the lampirs without the ring this afternoon. And the creatures still shied away from me. They were *scared* of me! And that's not all. . . One of the barons came to join the fight. And, well, my lip got cut and my blood dripped on to his arm. And then, he just sizzled and melted away – as if my blood was poison!"

Ben stopped walking and peered at Jack's mouth. He could see the cut in his friend's lip. It still looked sore and red.

"And that was when I put everything together in me mind," Jack went on. He hesitated, looking suddenly shy as they carried on up the rocky pathway. "Everyone thinks I'm Polish, don't they?" he said eventually. "Filip Cinska spoke to me in Polish the first time we met. And old Roza said she knew my face. And although I've always thought I was a Londoner through and through, I can't be sure, can I? I mean, I never knew me parents, so they could have come from anywhere. They might have been Polish. And if they were, that means I'm Polish too, by blood. And a Polish person who terrifies lampirs . . . well, that can mean only one thing. . ."

"It means that you must be a *dhampir*!" Ben murmured in amazement, feeling the hair lift on the back of his neck as he stared at Jack's familiar face.

"Exactly," said Jack. "And Emily, meanwhile, was

relying on my ring to protect her. And it let her down."

"But that's not your fault," Ben said firmly. He reached out and patted Jack on the shoulder. "It's no one's fault. And we shouldn't waste time trying to work out who's responsible for what. We should just hurry up and rescue Em before it's too late."

"You're right," Jack said with a nod. "I just thought you should know, that's all."

"I'm glad you told me," Ben said with a grin. He suddenly felt more hopeful than he had done for days. He was going to rescue his sister with a dhampir at his side – and dhampirs were the only people who had ever managed to defeat Count Casimir and his barons.

Castle Lampirska came into view around the next bend, and Ben caught his breath when he saw that every window shone with bright golden light. Even the walls seemed to be suffused with a supernatural glow, as if the black rocks from which the castle was built had come alive.

"Looks like 'is Lampir-ness is making 'imself at home," muttered Jack.

They made their way carefully across the repaired drawbridge and into the dark courtyard. The castle's enormous front door was wide open, a huge rectangle of golden light. Ben glanced at Jack, his eyebrows raised. Jack pressed his finger to his lips and they approached quietly, their feet barely making a sound on the smooth cobbles of the courtyard.

They came to a halt outside the front door, pressing themselves against the castle wall to one side of the entrance. Ben listened carefully, but he could hear only the music still drifting from within.

"What do you think?" he whispered to Jack.

"I think we go in," Jack replied.

Cautiously, the two boys crept inside. They were amazed to see that the great hall was a very different place to the deserted, dusty ruin they'd seen earlier. Flaming torches had been propped into wall-brackets and candles flickered on every surface. Light gleamed on the newly-polished gold and silver plates, and made the crystal goblets sparkle. The lampirs had obviously found another table from somewhere.

This is what it must have been like for the Lampirska family during their days of greatness, Ben thought, staring up at the huge, glittering chandeliers.

Suddenly, he felt Jack's hand grab the back of his jacket, and he found himself being jerked back behind a tall cupboard.

"Lampirs," Jack mouthed, pressing himself back against the wall.

Ben carefully peered out from behind the cupboard and saw a figure emerge from a narrow archway. The man was wearing a green doublet and hose, and a short cloak. An elaborate silver chain hung around his neck. The only sign that he was a lampir was the purplish blotching of his putrefying skin, and the glazed surface of his milky-white eyeballs. He was carrying a large silver tray, loaded with bowls of fruit and slices of meat fanned out on pure white plates.

Behind him came an exotic-looking pageboy in an Eastern-style costume. He also carried a tray, but one which rattled with crystal goblets and dusty bottles of wine. The young boy was a lampir too, but not long dead, Ben guessed, because his complexion was pink and unspoiled. As he passed beneath a flaming torch, the light caught a jewelled pin which sparkled at the front of his gold silk turban.

Together, the pair of lampirs made their way across the great hall and disappeared through another archway which led towards a grand marble staircase.

Where were they going? Ben wondered. The creatures had looked as though they were going to serve food and drink at a lavish banquet.

Ben glanced at Jack, and pointed in the direction the lampirs had gone. Jack nodded vigorously, obviously thinking along the same lines: they had to follow.

Quietly, the boys ran across the great hall and on through the archway. Keeping their heads low in case the lampirs looked back and caught a glimpse of them, they scuttled up the marble staircase. At the top, they found themselves at the end of a long corridor lined with doors.

There was no sign of the lampirs.

"Which way?" asked Jack in a frustrated whisper.

Ben caught a glimpse of the pageboy's robes as he disappeared around a corner halfway along the corridor. "There they go," he replied.

The friends hurried after them. It seemed as though they walked for ever, before they at last emerged into a magnificent hallway with a high ceiling. Red velvet curtains were looped back on either side of a giant marble archway, and beyond the archway was an enormous and splendid black-and-gold banqueting hall. Marble columns supported the vaulted ceiling where a thousand tiny candles sparkled like stars, and the candlelight shone down on a glossily-polished black dining table, which bowed under the weight of cutlery and candelabra.

Ben gaped. He'd been to several banquets back in London, but he'd never seen anything like this! The table was laden with food: quails' eggs layered with slices of orange, dishes of cream sprinkled with cinnamon and sugar crystals, a whole roast swan scattered with rose petals, pigeons, partridge, and a peacock with its tail feathers still in place. . .

"Blimey!" Jack muttered. "Ain't that a sight?"

Suddenly, Ben noticed that the lampir-man and the pageboy were coming back. Quickly, he and Jack hid behind one of the red velvet curtains until the lampirs had gone. Then they emerged and ventured cautiously into the banqueting hall.

The long left wall was taken up by a series of huge

arched doorways which gave out on to a large stone balcony. The doors were made of timber and glass, and had been propped open to allow an icy breeze to blow through the hall. Ben moved over to one of the doorways and peered outside. He saw a stone balustrade topped with a crust of snow, silver-white against the dark night sky. The balcony clearly overhung the mountainside, because through the balustrade Ben could see nothing but an interminable drop to the valley floor, where the frozen landscape was lit by moonlight. This part of the castle was so high up that wisps of cloud curled in the air around the balcony.

"Something's going on here tonight," Jack muttered, wandering over to join his friend.

"I'd say that's a safe bet," Ben agreed. He glanced around the banqueting hall again. Several doors led out of the room at either end, all of them closed. "I wonder where we should start looking for Emily?"

Even as he looked, one of the doors began to swing open and Ben's heart skipped a beat. "Someone's coming!" he hissed, and dragged Jack out on to the balcony where they ducked behind a stone urn. The darkness cloaked them, broken only by an elaborate, wrought-iron candelabra of flickering candles which stood in one corner of the balcony.

Ben peered cautiously back into the hall.

Count Casimir Lampirska strode across the room, the soles of his long chainmail boots ringing on the marble floor. He had changed his clothes since Ben had seen him last, and now he was even more lavishly dressed than before. His tunic was made of white satin encrusted with pearls and diamonds, the sleeves slashed to reveal black silk beneath. A jewelled belt was slung low around his hips, with a small, bejewelled silver dagger fastened at one side.

"Handsome fellow, ain't he?" Jack whispered dryly.

For a moment the count paused with his back to the balcony, surveying the long table in the middle of the room. Then he held up one hand – candlelight flashed on the rubies and emeralds in his rings – and snapped his fingers. Instantly a hundred lampir servants lurched into the room and gathered before him. They stood in rows; some dressed as exotically as the pageboy, others in little more than rags and half-rotten sheepskin coats. They stood before their master, their breath rasping between their fangs. Then they fell to their knees and each one touched a hand to his forehead, then clenched his fist over his heart in a gesture of allegiance.

Lampirska spoke to them in rapid-fire Polish, his powerful voice echoing up and down the hall. Ben glanced at Jack, who widened his eyes and shrugged. Neither of them could begin to guess what the count was saying.

But suddenly, he was speaking in English. "You may enter, my dear," he announced in a loud, clear voice, turning to face the door he himself had come through only moments before.

A young woman glided into the room and the count extended his hand towards her. She had her back to the balcony as she joined him and placed her slender fingers on his. Her long white gown shimmered as the count led her towards a huge carved throne at the head of the table.

Even watching from behind, Ben could tell that the young woman was beautiful. She moved with a serene grace, stepping elegantly across the marble floor. Her long hair had been brushed until it shone, and it curled loosely over her shoulders like a sheet of dark copper satin, perfectly framing her pale, oval face. . .

And it was then – as she turned around to take her place next to the count at the head of the table – that Ben recognized her. He put his hand over his mouth to stifle a cry of horror, as beside him, Jack turned pale.

The young woman, sitting so serenely at Count Lampirska's side, was Emily.

CHAPTER TWENTY-ONE

Jack gaped, unable to believe his eyes. He'd never seen Emily look quite like this before. She was no longer his sensible, no-nonsense, breeches-wearing friend, but a lovely young countess.

"She looks like a portrait we've got at home of our mama," Ben whispered, seemingly more to himself than to Jack. His face looked suddenly bleak, and Jack knew he was thinking about the mother he'd known all too briefly. Lavinia Cole had died when Ben and Emily were very small. And now Ben faced the possibility of losing his sister too.

Jack reached out and gave Ben's arm a comforting squeeze.

For a moment, the two boys watched as the count leaned over Emily, stroking her shoulder and speaking softly to her. Emily didn't respond. She stared out across the table blankly. She seemed oblivious of her surroundings.

"Do you think she's pretending?" Jack asked.

Ben shook his head. "I don't think so," he whispered back. "I think the count has hypnotized her."

Jack stared at his friend in astonishment. Then he turned to look at Emily again and decided that Ben was right. Emily was barely breathing. Her eyes were dull and vacant, and her hands lay motionless in her lap. She was mesmerized.

The realization revolted Jack. Rage boiled up inside him but he fought it down, letting a steely determination take its place.

"My dear," Count Lampirska was saying to Emily. "I will send for my barons at once!"

He strode across the room, and Jack knew with a sickening certainty that the count was heading for the balcony. He exchanged a horrified glance with Ben, and the two friends squeezed back even further behind the stone urn, making themselves as small and insignificant as possible.

Fortunately, the count didn't notice them. He was too intent on his purpose as he strode out into the cold night and approached the snow-capped balustrade. He stood beside the wrought-iron candelabra, lifted his arm and held his hand out, speaking Polish in a soft, coaxing voice.

All at once, something black flew out of the night sky. It fluttered above the balcony for a moment, and then landed on the count's outstretched hand. It was a bat. Its leathery wings rustled as it settled, and the flickering candlelight made its beady eyes glow red.

Lampirska whispered something to the bat and it promptly took off again, wheeling up into the moonlight before swooping away down the black mountainside.

The count went back inside, and a few minutes later, the sound of horses' hooves thundered across the drawbridge and clattered into the castle courtyard. Bridles rattled. Boots struck the flagstones. Then voices began to carry along the corridors. The barons had returned, summoned by their master.

They entered the banqueting hall in a group, laughing and slapping each other on the back. Five handsome young men dressed in luxurious velvets and silks with rich jewels sparkling on their fingers and at their throats.

The count introduced them to Emily in turn: "Barons Sigismund and Boleslav. . ." he said. "Vladislav, Lajos and Ladislas. . ."

The barons swept low in elaborate bows, and several of them jostled to be first to kiss Emily's hand.

Count Lampirska laughed as he stood at the head of the table. When the five barons had taken their places at the feast, he spread his arms wide. "Welcome back, my brothers. Tonight is a very special night, because we have in our midst a guest whose blood is young and strong – the blood of life!"

He turned to Emily and smiled down at her, his red lips slightly parted. Emily didn't respond, but just stared out across the table, obviously stupefied. "Miss Emily

Cole has consented to join us," the count continued. "So let the feast begin!"

With that, he sat, twitched back his cuff and drew his wrist up to his mouth. His sharp, perfect fangs glittered for a moment, and then disappeared as he sank them savagely into his own flesh. Appalled, Jack and Ben watched as the count reached for a jewelled goblet and pressed it to the puncture wounds.

The goblet slowly filled with blood that was so dark it was almost black.

The barons leaned forwards in their seats, whispering excitedly in Polish.

The Count raised a hand. "We will speak English tonight, in honour of our guest," he commanded.

For a moment, he tilted the goblet to the candlelight, inspecting the colour. Then he passed it to Emily.

"Drink!" he whispered.

The barons watched, rapt, as an entranced Emily took the goblet from the count's hand. Showing no emotion, or even any awareness of what she was doing, Emily slowly sipped and swallowed the blood.

Out on the balcony, Jack clapped his hand to his mouth in revulsion. He glanced at Ben, and saw that his friend had his hand on the knife at his belt. He looked as though he was about to dash into the banqueting hall and attack the count.

Jack put a steadying hand on his arm. *Not yet*, his warning look said to Ben. *Wait. . .*

Back in the banqueting hall, the barons were passing the jewelled goblet around the table now, each of them taking a sip of their master's blood before passing it on. Afterwards, they wiped their mouths with the backs of their hands and smacked their lips with obvious relish.

"My brothers," the count intoned, "I wish to express my sense of grief at the loss of our esteemed brother, Baron Ignatiuz." He gestured to the empty place halfway down the right-hand side of the table. "Ignatiuz was killed today at the hands of an infidel." There was a clamouring among the barons, but the count stilled them with a single gesture. "Rest assured that the infidel will pay for his crime," he continued. "And we, my brothers, will survive. Indeed we shall thrive! For we are the last of the Seven – and we have been set free!"

Baron Boleslav, a handsome man with a thin, straight nose and flowing golden hair, nodded and pounded the table with his fist. "All hail, Lampirska!" he declared. "Our Lord and Master!"

The other barons also pounded the table with their fists. "Lampirska! Lampirska!" they chanted.

Their voices swelled and soared, rising up to the vaulted ceiling. All around them, the lampir servants scurried this way and that. Bringing silver platters, bottles of wine and further dishes for the feast.

The count surveyed the servants fondly. "I am also delighted," he went on, cutting off the barons' chants, "that our descendants – these generations of lampirs created by the dark forces of my magic – have also woken to the sound of the bells! Even now they rampage across the countryside, spreading chaos and uncertainty." He nodded, still smiling. "And chaos and uncertainty are our friends, brothers, for in chaotic times we can venture out unopposed, to drink our fill from the fat of the land!"

"Blood is life!" the barons chorused.

The count waved his arms expansively at the loaded table. "Feast!" he commanded.

Immediately the barons fell upon the food, tearing the legs from roast ducks with their teeth and scooping up handfuls of oysters. At the head of the table, the count served Emily a delicate plate of quails' eggs and rose petals. She ate politely, still mesmerized.

Lampir waiters swarmed around the table, pouring wine into crystal goblets. The barons nodded and raised their glasses.

"From the cellars, Count?" asked Baron Vladislav, a bold-eyed young man in a sea-green tunic.

The Count nodded and smiled. "I believe you have a bottle of the 1443 there, Vladislav. A very good year, if I remember rightly."

Vladislav smiled and swigged more wine from his goblet. "An excellent year," he said with satisfaction. "The finest vintage."

And as the arch-lampirs drained their goblets and gestured to the waiters for more, the candlelight

194

gleamed through the crystal, making the contents glow crimson. Jack frowned, and then leaned closer to Ben. "That ain't wine," he whispered. "That's blood!"

"*What?*" Ben demanded incredulously, staring at the rich red liquid. "But they're getting drunk!"

And Ben was right. Across the banqueting hall, Baron Lajos snatched a bottle from one of the waiters and tore out the cork with his teeth. Laughing, he climbed up on his chair and stood unsteadily, slurping blood straight from the neck of the bottle. Around him, the other barons slowly clapped their hands and chanted their comrade's name, "Lajos! Lajos! Lajos!"

Once the bottle was drained, Baron Lajos wiped his cuff across his mouth, smearing blood on to his cheek. Then, with an exultant cry, he jumped down from his chair and dashed the bottle to the marble floor where it shattered into a million pieces.

Jack's stomach turned over. The barons were indeed drunk – on blood!

"And now," exclaimed the count, rising to his feet. "We come to the high point of the evening." He seized Emily's hand and bowed low over it, pressing his lips to her skin in a kiss which seemed to last for ever.

At last he looked up into her vacant eyes. "Tonight, my dear, we will drink the most precious blood of all. The blood of life. . ." His eyes glittered darkly. "*Your* blood."

CHAPTER TWENTY-TWO

At the count's words, Emily smiled in a vacant way. It made Ben feel sick to see her like that – she had no idea of the fate that lay in store for her.

Beside him, Jack had reached out to Ben and was frantically tearing at his shirt sleeves. Ben suddenly realized that his friend was trying to rip his clothes to shreds.

"What are you doing?" he hissed.

But Jack was too busy now making ribbons of Ben's trousers to reply. His fingers worked fast, tearing fabric and unpicking seams.

Ben silently handed him his knife. "Here," he muttered. "Whatever you're doing, do it with this. And then please tell me what you're up to."

Jack took the knife and grinned, testing the blade against his thumb. Satisfied that it was sharp, he turned it round and handed the hilt back to Ben.

"You're going to have to cut me," he said simply.

Ben goggled at his friend. "Have you gone mad?"

"No," Jack responded with a grin. "I've never been saner in me life. It's how we'll save Emily. We'll poison the lampirs with some of my dhampir blood!"

Ben's mind cleared. "I see," he said. "But why have you ripped my clothes?"

"Because you're going to have to disguise yourself as a lampir, and go out there and serve the poisoned blood. I can't do it: the count has already seen me far too clearly," Jack explained hurriedly.

Ben nodded.

"So it has to be you," Jack continued. "They're all drunk, so as long as you do a good impression of a lampir, we should get away with it."

"Will drinking your blood be enough to destroy them?" Ben asked.

Jack shrugged. "I can't be sure," he said soberly. "But I saw what it did to Baron Ignatiuz when one drop touched his flesh. If drinking it has only half the effect, it will reduce them all to a pile of cinders."

Ben nodded enthusiastically. "All right," he said. "I'll act like a lampir servant and serve your blood."

He glanced around the balcony, wondering whether there was anything else which would help his disguise. One of the candles in the candelabra had guttered and gone out. It gave him an idea. He reached out and rubbed his thumb against the blackened wick, then smeared soot beneath his eyes to make them look hollow.

"Looks good," Jack said with a nod. He'd been scraping his hands along the floor of the balcony, scooping up bits of moss and dead leaves. He rubbed them in Ben's hair and then sat back on his heels to check his handiwork.

"Now all we need is your blood," Ben said reluctantly.

"We need something to collect it in first," Jack muttered. He peered out from behind the stone urn and watched as the count called for more "wine" to be served. The barons were all gazing at Emily with barely-concealed anticipation now. They were hungry for her blood.

One of the lampir waiters came shuffling past the open doors which gave on to the balcony.

Ben and Jack exchanged a knowing glance. . .

Then, together, they pounced. They took the lampir by surprise, wrestling him quickly to the ground, and dragging him behind the stone urn. Jack delivered a sharp blow to the creature's temple which momentarily stunned him, while Ben plucked the bottle from his clawed hands.

No sooner was the bottle in their possession, than the two boys hefted the lampir right over the balustrade. There was a muted cry as he plunged headlong into the abyss below.

Ben and Jack crouched back behind the urn. Jack held his arm out again and nodded firmly. "Now, cut me," he said softly.

Holding his breath, Ben placed the sharp blade against his friend's arm and cut the skin. Crimson blood sprang to the surface like a string of small rubies.

Jack gritted his teeth and squeezed the flesh. "Cut some more," he whispered. "We need the blood to flow freely so we can get it into the bottle."

Ben did as he was asked, and soon Jack's precious dhampir blood was spilling into the neck of the wine bottle. Then, Ben used a strip of his torn trousers to bandage Jack's wound. And at last, they were ready.

Ben stood up and prepared to walk out into the banqueting hall. He hesitated for a moment. What would happen to Emily if he failed to fool the arch-lampirs and was caught? He had to do this right. He swallowed hard and remembered their great friend Filip Cinska, who had taught them how to do impressions of the lampir death rattle by swigging Polish tea. There was no Polish tea, but Ben remembered the noise perfectly. It was a low, guttural growl, deep in the throat.

He stepped out into the banqueting hall, into the blazing light from a thousand candles, growling and rolling his eyes up into his head.

"At last!" the count said lazily, beckoning Ben. "When I say serve the wine, brother, I mean now, not later. Hurry up! Our goblets have been empty too long!"

Ben shuffled around the table, tilting the wine bottle over each glass and pouring poisoned blood for each of the barons.

First Baron Vladislav. Then Sigismund. Then he reached the head of the table and poured for Emily and the count.

"More!" urged the count. "Give me more!"

Ben poured obediently, filling the count's crystal goblet to the rim.

"Good," Lampirska said with a satisfied smile.

Ben uttered a low, guttural groan and moved on to Baron Boleslav and, finally, Baron Ladislas.

As he poured for Baron Ladislas, Ben's hand trembled slightly. The neck of the bottle clinked against the rim of Ladislas's crystal goblet.

Abruptly Ladislas shot out his fist and gripped Ben's wrist with such force that Ben almost dropped the bottle.

"I've not seen you before," the young baron snarled, his eyes focused on Ben's face.

Heart pounding, Ben rolled his eyes further up into his head.

"Leave him alone, Ladislas," said one of the other barons in a mocking tone. "He's only young. . . Probably one of Ignatiuz's!"

"But he's new," insisted Ladislas. "And you know how newness intrigues me."

"Boring!" yelled Lajos drunkenly, waving his goblet in the air. "Let him pour the wine. It's my turn. My goblet's still empty!"

But Ladislas was still staring up at Ben's face. Ben

forced himself to breathe, rasping the air between his teeth and praying that it sounded as if he had fangs.

At last, Ladislas let go of his wrist with a disgusted snort. "Have him then, Lajos," he snarled. "And much good may he do you!"

Forcing himself to stay calm, Ben poured the last goblet of "wine" and shuffled back across the room. He walked slowly past the entrance to the balcony, and with a quick glance to check that none of the arch-lampirs was watching, he slipped back out to rejoin Jack.

The two boys crouched in the shadows and waited. . .

The count rose to his feet and held his goblet high. "Blood is life!" he exclaimed, his voice echoing around the hall.

The barons hauled themselves drunkenly to their feet as well. "Lampirska!" they all responded, their voices rising as one.

All six drank deeply, draining their goblets. Then, one by one, they tossed the glasses backwards over their shoulders so that the crystal shattered on impact with the marble floor.

Ben and Jack watched breathlessly. At first nothing happened. Then Baron Lajos staggered slightly and clutched at his throat.

The others laughed, obviously thinking he was making some drunken joke.

But then Ladislas turned pale and gripped the edge of the table. "*It . . . hurts. . .*" he gasped.

And suddenly all five barons were howling with pain, clutching at their throats and stomachs. Their skin began to split open in dozens of cracks. Rivulets of fire chased along the edges of the tiny fissures, and the stench of scorching flesh filled the air.

Count Lampirska stared at his barons in horror and confusion. "What is happening?" he roared, an edge of panic to his voice.

But the barons could not reply – they were too busy screaming in agony. Baron Ladislas was clenching his fists, hammering them on the tabletop so that goblets juddered and ice sculptures toppled. Sigismund and Vladislav began to pluck at their own skin, pulling off great handfuls of scorched, burnt flesh.

The barons' eyes bulged as their skin turned to ash, falling away to reveal the muscles and sinews beneath. Then they too were gone, and only the bones were left, stark and white. But only for a moment, because they also burned, until all five bodies collapsed into piles of grey and silver ash.

Abruptly, Lampirska clenched his fists, threw his head back in pain and flung his arms wide. His black hair rippled down his back. Ben could see a ball of light burning outwards from the count's chest. It scorched his white tunic as it grew larger and larger. A thousand cracks chased each other upwards and outwards, splitting the count's skin into burning fissures that flashed and sparked.

Agony was etched across Lampirska's handsome face and he let out a terrible cry that shook even the foundations of the castle. The vaulted ceiling cracked from side to side, and slabs of stone fell in a shower of dust. The count's cry became a howl. The sound was deafening, and with it came a build-up of pressure in the air – a dark force that seemed to press down on the castle from above. Shrieking sounds, like lost souls in torment, seemed to echo from the very rock that formed the castle's walls.

Out on the balcony, Ben and Jack crouched with their hands over their ears, trying to block out the terrible din. The earth rumbled and shook.

Jack nudged Ben with his elbow and pointed at Count Lampirska. "He's disintegrating!" he yelled above the noise.

Ben stared as fire ran outwards from Casimir Lampirska's chest, shimmering along his limbs which were turning quickly to ash. Tiny flames rippled up his neck.

For a moment, his eyes widened, so that they were like the bottomless black pits of hell. Then with a last roar of rage, Count Casimir Lampirska imploded in a shower of ash.

Beside him, Emily blinked as a handful of cinders landed in her lap.

CHAPTER TWENTY-THREE

Jack leaped to his feet as the earth beneath him began to vibrate. The castle walls rumbled and split. Great cracks appeared in the black rock. Beside Jack, the stone urn shook and teetered. Finally it toppled over, smashing on to the floor of the balcony.

"We have to get out of here," Jack shouted to Ben. "The whole place is going to go!"

No sooner had he uttered the words, than a deafening thunderclap ripped the night air. The balcony cracked wide open, and Jack caught a glimpse of the chasm beneath.

"Run!" Ben yelled.

The boys launched themselves into the banqueting hall. But the crack followed them, widening as it chased across the marble floor. All around them rocks fell and masonry crumbled. Dust and debris rained down as the castle began to collapse.

Emily was on her feet at the head of the table. "What's

happening?" she cried. She still looked slightly dazed, but she seemed more herself again. Jack guessed that she had been released from the count's spell, though she probably had no memory of the past few hours.

There was no time to explain. He and Ben raced over to her and took an arm each. "Come on, Em!" Ben cried, tugging her out from behind the table.

Together, the three friends ran for their lives, out through the marble archway and down the long hall. But the way was blocked! Dying lampirs lay heaped across their path, groaning and scraping at the flagstones with their long black nails.

The friends skidded to a halt and began to back away. The nearest lampir gazed up at them, growled deep in its throat, and began to drag itself along the floor towards them.

"We have to go back," Ben said desperately.

"No, this way!" Emily exclaimed. Seizing their sleeves, she dragged Ben and Jack through a half-open door and down a flight of narrow, twisting stairs. Halfway down there was a torch propped in a wall-bracket.

"Wait!" said Jack, quickly reaching to pluck the torch from its bracket. "We'll use this to light our way."

With the torch firmly held out in front, the three hurtled on down the stairs. At the bottom of the staircase, there were three passageways.

"This place is like a maze," muttered Ben. "Which way now?"

"This way," said Emily firmly, taking the left-most fork.

Jack exchanged a puzzled glance with Ben. "How do you know that, Em?" he asked.

"I'm not really sure . . . I just know," she replied, and led them through a maze of stone corridors and flights of stairs that cracked and crumbled beneath their feet as they ran.

All around them, stone rained down upon stone. The torch guttered and flared in Jack's hand, and he prayed it wouldn't go out.

Suddenly, they emerged into an empty chamber that seemed to lead nowhere.

Jack frowned and stared about the room, completely disorientated. He felt a wave of panic. "Where are we?" he asked.

"Don't know," Ben muttered. "But this isn't the way out. Let's go back."

But even as they turned to leave, a huge roaring sound almost deafened them. Thunder rumbled through the night air, and the entrance to the chamber seemed to explode. Flying masonry spewed outwards, and Jack threw an arm up to protect his face. Together, the boys shoved Emily down and crouched over her. Jack felt sharp stones raining on to his back.

When the roaring stopped, Jack raised his head

cautiously. His torch had gone out, so the chamber was now as black as midnight. Wiping the dust from his eyes, Jack squinted across the room, trying to make out whether the doorway was blocked.

Emily coughed and sat up. "I can't see," she whispered.

But just then, a shaft of silvery moonlight slanted across the room from a crack high in the ceiling. It shed enough light to confirm Jack's worst fears – the door to the stone chamber had completely disappeared, replaced by a torrent of fallen rocks.

"We're trapped," Jack muttered.

But Ben was frantically looking round for another exit. "The window!" he cried, and took off across the room.

The shaft of moonlight disappeared, hidden by clouds, and abruptly they were plunged into darkness again.

"Can't see a thing," muttered Ben angrily. Jack heard him staggering over fallen rocks in the direction of the window.

"Be careful," Jack said. "We don't know what's below it."

"I'm fairly sure we're on the opposite side of the castle from the banqueting hall," Ben reasoned. "And we've come down a long way. We should be able to climb down from here."

"Don't do anything until the moon comes out from behind that cloud," Jack warned. He held tight to Emily's hand as he picked his way across the room, trying to follow the sound of Ben's voice in the darkness. He could see the window now – a dim rectangle of slightly lighter black against the pitch darkness of the castle walls.

"I'm at the window," Ben said. "I'm just going to climb out. Hold on. . ."

Suddenly, Jack felt Emily's hand slip from his. With a muted cry, she leaped forwards and seized the collar of Ben's shirt, dragging him backwards.

"Wha—" gasped Ben, staggering back from the window, as the clouds cleared and the room was flooded with moonlight.

Jack stumbled to the window and peered out. He saw nothing but a sheer precipice which plummeted thousands of metres to the valley floor below. If Ben had climbed out of the window, he would have plunged to his death!

Ben looked out too. Then both boys turned to stare at Emily in amazement.

"How did you know?" Jack asked incredulously.

Emily bit her lip. "I know the whole castle. . ." she said hesitantly. "It's as if I lived here years ago. I can remember things." She glanced around the ruined chamber. "This was a nursery once," she said softly, her face full of sadness. "I can recall the day the servants closed it up, after the little boy died. . ." She shook her head as if to clear it. "That was a long time ago," she added. "Centuries ago!"

Jack and Ben exchanged a puzzled glance.

Emily stared past them both and Jack turned to see what she was looking at. A tapestry hung askew on one of the walls. Its faded silks depicted a woodland scene of baby deer and tiny red squirrels. Jack guessed that it might have been suitable for a nursery. He frowned. Was Emily right? Did she have memories of how the castle had been, long ago? And if so, how?

The castle was still shaking around them. Another piece of rock fell from the ceiling. Emily tucked up the skirts of her long gown, and then picked her way across the room towards the tapestry. "This is the way out," she said abruptly. And she lifted a corner of the tapestry to reveal a small door. It swung open easily, and beyond was a flight of spiral stairs that wound down through the castle and came out in a corner of the kitchens.

"Come on," Emily whispered, and without hesitation she led them out through the scullery, past the stone well, and into the main courtyard.

The castle was still crumbling all around them. Rocks rained down into the courtyard and tumbled over the edge of the ravine. Looking up, Jack saw that high above them, dozens of bats wheeled and circled in the night sky, black against the silvery moon.

He shuddered and dashed onwards with Ben and Emily at his side. They raced across the drawbridge, feeling the timber shiver and shake beneath their feet.

"Faster!" gasped Emily, and moments later they were

across, their feet striking the solid rock on the other side of the ravine.

Behind them a great cracking sound tore the air. They all turned to see that a huge rift had appeared at the base of one of the watchtowers. The tower teetered for a moment, black against the night sky. Then finally it toppled like a felled tree, smashing down through the drawbridge and obliterating it completely.

Jack gaped. They had made it across just in time!

Eventually the shaking stopped. The earth fell still. The dust began to settle.

The three friends looked at each other and then slowly lifted their eyes to stare at the castle. . .

Except that there *was* no castle.

The turrets and spires had all gone. In their place was a jumbled mass of boulders and rubble. Silvery moonlight slanted down on the ruins, casting deep, velvety shadows into the heaps of tumbled rock.

Count Casimir and his barons were dead, and Castle Lampirska had been destroyed.

"We were lucky to get out of there alive," Jack muttered. "A few minutes later, and we'd have been crushed beneath all them rocks!"

Emily's white gown was torn and ragged, her hair tangled. She was already holding Ben's hand, but now she turned to Jack. He grinned down at her, and she smiled back as she curled her dusty fingers into his.

All three of them stood for a moment, surveying the

scene. Then, still holding hands, they turned and began to make their way down the mountainside.

Behind them a plume of dust rose from the ruins of Casimir Lampirska's castle, and drifted across the moon.

The lampir plague was over.

EPILOGUE

Grinning, Jack held out his glass for some more of Yelena's hot apple cider.

"Steady, Jack," Edwin Sherwood said with a chuckle. "We don't want a drunkard on our hands!"

Ben and Emily laughed, too. All three of the friends were sitting around a roaring log fire in Pavel's house, warm and safe. Edwin was propped in an armchair with a fur rug tucked around his knees. Thick bandages were just visible in the neckline of his shirt. He was pale, but cheerful, and had been delighted and relieved when Jack, Ben and Emily had made it back to the village earlier that day.

After a long, cold journey down the mountain, the friends had arrived in Ornak at dawn. All of them were exhausted, parched with thirst, and footsore. But now, after a long sleep and hot baths, they had gathered with the villagers to tell their story. They paused every now and then to sip hot apple cider while Brother Lubek translated their talc.

"So the count and his barons are truly gone?" Pavel said, smoothing his black moustache with one hand. "That is the best news I have ever heard!"

Yelena smiled widely and said something in Polish.

"She says you three are heroes," Lubek told them.

While the villagers had been hearing all about the final defeat of lampirism, old Roza had been gazing thoughtfully at Emily. Now she sat forwards in her rocking chair. "I think I know why you had such strong memories of the castle," she announced, her words translated by Brother Lubek. "It was because you drank some of Count Casimir's blood!"

Emily frowned thoughtfully. "Yes . . . that would make sense. . ." she said slowly. Her face cleared. "After the count drank my blood, he seemed to know all about *my* past. So it stands to reason that if I drank his, I would know about *his* past," she said, looking relieved that that particular mystery was finally solved.

Ben was perched on a stool at Edwin's side, with little Florian cross-legged on the floor at his feet, gazing up at him with a happy smile on his face. Florian's mother, Daria, hovered nearby, the embroidered hem of her long skirt swaying as she passed round some freshly-baked *bialys*.

"I'm glad you all managed to get down the mountain safely," Ben said, glancing across at Brother Lubek.

"I was a bit worried that the barons might have caught up with you!"

"I think they would have done," Brother Lubek said. "Those shadow-horses move fast! But halfway down the mountainside they stopped following us for some reason. Suddenly, they simply veered away and galloped back up the track."

"That's probably because the count sent a black bat down to summon them back to the castle," Jack said with a nod. He glanced up to find that old Roza had moved on from her contemplation of Emily, and was now looking straight at him. He smiled.

Roza smiled back. "I have something for you," she said.

As Brother Lubek translated her words, Roza reached a hand into her apron pocket. Shyly, she held out a small square of wood about the size of her palm. Jack took it and turned it over in his hands. It was a portrait, he realized, a miniature painted in oil on a canvas background.

But his heart started to pound as he looked at the picture – because the face that stared up out of the portrait was his own; dark brown hair, thin face, blue eyes. And yet it *couldn't* be him, because this face belonged to someone older than he was. Jack frowned and examined the portrait more closely, guessing that the man must be in his early twenties.

Jack became aware of Emily peering over his shoulder.

"It's you, Jack!" she said in amazement. "It's you in ten years' time!"

"Let me see. . ." Ben peered at the little portrait, and then he too looked amazed. "That man's your double!" he said, aiming a light-hearted punch at Jack's shoulder.

Jack looked across at Roza, puzzled. "Who is it?" he asked.

The old woman rocked her chair back and forth for a moment. The smile on her face told Jack that she was enjoying this moment very much.

"The man in the portrait is Stefan Kowalski," she said. "He was the last of the dhampir line in Ornak, and you will remember that he left here with his wife, Celestina, and his unborn child. . ."

As Brother Lubek translated Roza's words, Jack stared down at the picture again, at Stefan Kowalski's lean, handsome face and cheerful blue eyes. "Roza, are you saying that you think *I* was the unborn baby?" he asked, hardly able to breathe.

Old Roza simply nodded, still rocking back and forth in her chair as she smiled broadly at Jack. "It is plain to see," she said simply. "You are the image of your father, Jack."

And then suddenly *everyone* was smiling. Emily hugged Jack and he grinned at her shyly. Edwin shook his hand. Ben grinned and gave him a thumbs up sign.

Pavel reached out and clapped Jack on the back.

"Welcome home, boy!" he cried with a shout of laughter. "Welcome home!"

Yelena poured more hot apple cider for everyone and Brother Lubek proposed a toast.

"To Jack Harkett!" everyone bellowed.

"But he's really Jack Kowalski!" Ben pointed out, laughing.

Emily reached out a hand and touched Jack's arm. "I suppose this means you'll want to stay here in Poland?" she asked, looking a little sad. "There must be so much you want to find out about your family and heritage."

Jack thought for a moment about the mother and father he'd never known: Stefan and Celestina. They'd had other children before him, brothers and sisters of Jack's who had fallen victim to lampir raids – that was what had made the Kowalskis leave Ornak.

If the couple had lived, perhaps they would have ended up in London. And Jack might still have grown up in the East End, near the docks which had been the constant backdrop of his childhood, and which still felt like home to him.

"Nah," Jack said to Emily at last. "I've been Jack Harkett all me life. And Jack Harkett I'll stay. Besides," he looked at Emily and Ben, and Edwin Sherwood, "you're me family now. And London is me home. Always has been and always will be!"

"But you will *always* be welcome in Ornak," said

Pavel firmly. And everyone raised their glasses to that and cheered loudly.

Then Daria spoke in Polish, and Brother Lubek translated. "She is asking how long you intend to stay here before you return to England?" he said.

The friends all looked at Edwin, who grinned and eased his injured arm.

"I should be fit enough to travel in a few days," the archaeologist said. "I must admit that I'm looking forward to going home. And when I get there. . ." he added with a chuckle, "I think I shall stay put for a while. Every time I go globetrotting, I encounter nothing but blood-sucking demons and mortal peril!"

Jack, Ben and Emily looked at each other and grinned. They were all inclined to agree!